hey,
Dummy

ALSO BY KIN PLATT

Juvenile
   Big Max
   The Blue Man
   Sinbad and Me
   The Boy Who Could Make Himself Disappear
   Mystery of the Witch Who Wouldn't

Adult
   The Pushbutton Butterfly
   The Kissing Gourami

hey,
Dummy

by Kin Platt

CHILTON BOOK COMPANY

Philadelphia   New York   London

for Anne Einselen

hey,
Dummy

Out.   Go out.   Me . . .   Walk . . . . .
Nice.   Stoplook . . .   Pretty.   Things.
This.   This thing.   Oh nice thing.

Walk.   More walk.   Oh look . . .
Boys.
One boy.   One more boy.   One other more boy.
Play play on green green . . .
Touch.   Oh nice grass.   Soft green nice.

Boys play . . . . . .   play-play-play.   Throw what?
Run . . .   throw what . . .   catch-run-fall-play . . .
Talk.   Happy loud talk-talk.
One boy.   Kick.   Kick what?
Up. . .   Look up. . .   Sky.   Up in blue sky the what.
Fall.   Falling.   The what.
Funny fall the what.   Fall-fall over over this-that-way
the what. . .

Nice.   Nice what.   Nice funny what. . .
Smell.   Nice.   Hard.   Me . . . mine . . . my
Funny what.   Run.   Run-run-run-fall . . .
Oh oh my.
Boys.   Sit on.   Mad eyes, boys.   Hit.   Oh.
Hurt.   Kick.   Talk-talk . . .
Hurt.
My . . .   My funny what.   Hard long what.
Boys run play . . . funny what . . . my . . . my . . . what.
One.
One-two-three.
One.   One.

Go away from what my-funny-long-throwkick. . . . .
Hurt.
Why hurt mad-look   my funny throwkick?

1

A new kid moved into our neighborhood. Nobody knew his name. I was the first to call him Dummy and that name seems to have stuck.

It happened one afternoon after school. Charley, Dave and I were playing football on the corner lot. There weren't enough for a real game so we played two on one. Charley would center and snap the football to me, then run out and cut back for my pass. Dave was the other side. He had to watch Charley and me and try to break up the play. If he couldn't intercept the pass, he had to catch Charley before he ran over the line and scored. Dave could touch-tackle him or tackle him, depending on how he felt.

We had four downs to make it. After that, whoever

3

scored kicked off to the other two, the one who caught the ball becoming the new quarterback. We took turns at being center, quarterback, or defending the goal. We were just fooling around, throwing the ball, doing a lot of yelling, chasing after each other. It didn't mean a thing. I mean, what kind of football is three-man football?

To break the monotony I called punt formation. Charley snapped the ball and I kicked it, Dave playing far back as safety man. It gave him a chance to run the ball back after he caught it, and Charley and me a chance to tackle him. I didn't get off a good kick. The ball squirted high off the side of my foot, falling out of bounds, then taking a couple of crazy bounces and landing where some kid we hadn't noticed before was standing.

He picked it up and kept on looking at it, turning it over in his hands, trying to read what the label said. It was almost like he'd never seen a football before in his life.

I got annoyed waiting. "Hey Dummy," I yelled. "Throw the ball back."

He looked at me, then back at the football.

I waved my arm in a throwing motion. "Throw it back, will you?"

He just stood there, rolling it over in his hands, looking at all sides.

Charley, annoyed too, picked the name up from me. "Come on, Dummy. Throw the ball back."

The kid looked up at Charley, then back at the ball.

4

He turned it over and then held it close to his face, like he was going to try to eat it.

Dave started to run across the grass. "Pete's sake!" he yelled. "Give us the ball, dumbhead."

The kid took his eyes off the ball when Dave went charging over. I guess he panicked, because he did the dumbest thing possible—he hugged the ball close and started to run off with it.

"What's he doing?" I muttered crossly, running diagonally across the field to cut him off, waving my arms and yelling, "Throw it back, Dummy!"

He was chunky and heavy set, a rotten runner, moving like lead. Apart from that he never had a chance, because there were three of us, Dave and I are very fast, and the dumb kid kept running in a straight line, lumbering like a truck.

We converged on him like a three-pronged arrow. Dave hit him first in a good flying tackle across the knees. I came in around the chest and shoulders. Charley dived in from the side, and we all went down with a thud. Sitting on his chest I grabbed the ball away.

"What are you? Some kind of wise guy?"

He looked up at me kind of dumb.

I slapped him across the face.

"Aaah!" he said.

"Well, don't try that again or you'll get more," I told him.

He didn't say anything and I got up. The kid just lay there. Dave and Charley got up, too. Dave kicked him.

"There's one from me you can remember."

The kid didn't answer. There was a strange expression in his blue eyes, almost as if he was a foreigner and didn't understand our language. Charley, standing behind the kid's head, stepped one foot on the upturned face, leaving his sneaker mark on the Dummy's forehead.

"I'm branding you a football rustler," Charley said. "Now everybody will know."

Charley's got a wild sense of humor, and we all doubled up laughing. Then we ran across the lot to continue our game. I glanced back at the kid. He was still lying there. I wondered was he hurt or something. Then I wondered why he just took the punishment instead of fighting back or getting mad. He'd had the three of us against him, of course, but he was bigger and huskier than we were, and looked to be a little older, maybe thirteen.

"Come on, Dummy!" Charley yelled at me. "Throw the ball, will you?"

It broke us all up again. I tossed the ball high. Charley caught it, and Dave and I ganged up to tackle him. When I got to my feet I looked back to where the Dummy had been lying.

He was gone.

The final score was 7 for Charley, 9 for Dave and 4 for me. Thinking about that Dummy just lying there and saying "Aaaah!" after I hit him ruined my game.

Walk outside...
Light.   Pretty light.   Red nice light.
Walk.......

Oh.
Honk.   Honkhonkhonk.   Honkhonkhonkhonk.
Mad honk.   Stop.   Cars.
Honk-Cars ...   Screech ... honkhonk ...
Oh.
Mad-yell-honkhonk-screech-man   mad yell car.

Boy. Number one boy. My funny what-long-throw-
kick-boy   hit   hurt.
Talk.   Walk.......
Boy walk nice   honk-honk-honk
Talk.
No more boy.

The next time I saw the Dummy he was standing in the middle of the street watching the cars go by. There was a lot of traffic coming at him from both sides. He didn't look worried or nervous but he wasn't making any effort to cross to either side. He rocked back and forth, staying in one spot, a big goofy smile on his face. A car slowed up for him. When the Dummy didn't try to cross the driver got mad, honked his horn and zoomed past. Another came along, stopped, got tired of waiting, too, then like the first one honked his horn and tore past, yelling at the kid. He smiled.

I got nervous watching, walked out and tapped his shoulder.

"Hey," I said, "you trying to get yourself killed?"

He turned, looking puzzled. He frowned, rubbed his face, then smiled suddenly.

"Aaaah!"

I didn't like that "aaaah" sound again.

"You okay?" I asked.

The smile seemed to be pasted on his face. "Aaaah," he said.

8

Pete's sake! Maybe he really is a dummy.

"Is that all you can say?" I asked him.

He rocked back on his heels and thought about it. Two more cars came up from opposite sides and started honking. I grabbed the Dummy's arm.

"Come on. Let's continue this interesting conversation where it's safe."

He let me pull him across to the curb. The cars that had waited honked at us to get even. I faced the kid on the sidewalk.

"What's with you? Can't you talk?"

His head bobbed cheerfully. "Aaaah!" he said.

I wondered was he kidding, and glanced at him suspiciously. He was smiling, looking like he couldn't kid anybody if his life depended on it. I shook my head.

"Forget I mentioned it. So long."

I half expected him to come trotting after me, and looked back over my shoulder. He was standing where I had left him. His head bobbed. I saw his lips move but didn't hear anything.

He was probably still saying, "Aaah! Aaaah!"

2

My kid sister Susie is small and thin and very bright. She goes through periods where she gets tired of being herself.

One evening when she was alone in her room she let out this God-awful scream. My pop dropped his pipe and had to slap the hot ashes off his pants. My mom went two shades whiter. We ran inside to see was she getting herself murdered, and found her walking stooped over, a bath towel completely covering her head.

"Don't talk to me," she said. "I'm Marie Antoinette and they just chopped off my head."

My pop looked at her, then down at the holes in his new pants from the hot sparks of his pipe. He hauled off and smacked her fanny, hard. "That's a nice trick to pull on us!"

My mom pulled the towel off Susie's head and slapped her face. "How can you scare us like that!"

Susie clenched her fists and danced up and down. "Us—us!" she screamed back. "That's all you people think of. What about me with my head all chopped off?"

I laughed. My folks looked down at me like I was the loony one and walked out of her room.

"Why did they chop your head off?" I asked Susie.

"Because I know too much."

"Know too much about what?"

"Everything."

I looked at her but didn't ask her any more questions. I was used to her happenings, but somehow never able to avoid being caught up in them. Like the time she was sitting on the sofa of the living room, saw me walk in and held up her hand.

"Look out," she said. "Don't step on me—I'm an ant."

I shrugged. "Okay."

I sat down on the far end of the sofa and she screamed. Chairs scraped in the kitchen and my mom and pop rushed into the room.

"I never touched her," I said quickly.

"You did, too," my sister said. "I'm a big ant and you sat on part of me."

My pop couldn't seem to make up his mind which one to sock, Susie or me. His lip curled, his nose twitched, and his face got very red. For a long moment he looked just like those dumb fathers they show on the TV comedy shows. I don't get along too good with my folks, especially my pop, but for once I felt sorry for him. He finally let out a long sigh, turned and walked across the room, picked up his newspaper and sat down, snapping out the sports section.

"I wish I had her imagination," he said finally. "It might help me with the bills."

"How's that, Frank?" asked my mother.

"Say I'm a spider. Who would sue me?"

Mom nodded. "You've got a point there."

Susie was smart enough not to drive the teachers batty at school. It was like she had a spare personality there, something she could put on for the occasion. Once, after a parent-teacher conference, my mom came home shaking her head.

"What's wrong?" my pop asked.

"Miss Bond says she's no problem and relates wonderfully to everybody."

He lowered his newspaper. "Who said that?"

Mom gestured vaguely. "Her room teacher. Everybody at school."

"Give her a little time," he said. "She needs a little more time to get them all set up. Then—whammie!"

"I suppose so," my mom said uncertainly. "But isn't it odd that she just gives us those looks into her fantasy world?"

Pop shook his head. "Not odd at all," he said. "It's simple. She trusts us. She knows we won't kill her for those crazy things."

"I suppose," Mom said. "As long as she's good at school, and gets along, that's the main thing."

I cleared my throat.

"What's on your mind?" he asked, "or what passes for a mind?"

"You don't have to worry about Susie," I said, secretly shrugging off his scorn. "She makes everybody like her. It's like she has this magic spell over everybody."

Pop grunted something and then snapped out his paper. "Too bad some of that can't rub off on you."

"What's that mean?" I asked.

He baited me with his crooked grin.

"Tonight's your allowance night, isn't it?"

"Yeah," I said, puzzled.

"I happen to be broke," he said. "Good luck."

I shrugged and turned away. "Okay. If you're broke, you're broke."

He banged his fist down on the arm of his chair, threw his newspaper on the floor and got up. "That's what I mean," he yelled. "You give in too easily. Danny would have . . ."

Danny was my older brother who died when I was a baby.

I looked at my pop, waiting for him to finish, and he got madder still. Then he stuck his hand into his pocket and drew out a roll of bills. He peeled two dollars off and slapped them down on the coffee table.

"Okay," he said. "Okay." Then he walked out of the room.

I turned to my mom. "Now what did I do?"

"I guess he wants you to act like a man," she said. "You should try harder."

"But he said he was broke."

"Well," she said, "that's just a figure of speech with your father. He always says that."

"You mean he'd like it better if I made a stink about it?"

Mom shrugged. "To each his own," she said. "Now pick up your allowance money or I'll try to borrow some of it myself."

"It's only two bucks. What could you do with two bucks?"

"I really don't know," she said. "Maybe I'll think of something."

I pushed the money toward her. "Okay. If you need it, take it."

She frowned. "I was afraid of that. All right, Neil. Pick it up. Take your money."

I turned away. "I don't want it now. That money has a curse on it."

She reached out, grabbed my sleeve, and yanked me back.

"Pick up your money, Neil," she said sharply. "People used to be able to buy a very nice dinner in a good restaurant for just two dollars. It was worth something when your father and I were just married."

"That was a hundred years ago," I said. "What's that got to do with now?"

"I know all about now," she said. "But we have to

show some respect for the dear, dead, and departed. Take your money."

I had the feeling I'd reached the point of no return on that particular argument, which somehow was tied up with Danny. I took the money.

Me.   *Out* . . .

                              up . . .

Things.   *Look.*   *Look*   *down*

                                          look . . .

Ah place.   *Me.*   *Mine.*

Take nice soft for mouth

More   *nice*   *soft* . . .

Boy.   *The hit-boy my funny-what-throwkick.*

Car   *boy*   *street*   *honkhonk*

Cross-to-other . . .

talk-talk . . .

No want my   *soft*   *nice.*

3

It was still light enough to play some ball but the guys weren't on the lot. I waited around awhile and then decided I might as well get started breaking in my allowance.

I passed the record shop and the drug store, and by the time I reached the bakery my willpower was shot. I almost drooled looking at all those cakes inside.

I thought I was the only customer. Then I saw him. The Dummy. He was on the other side, his back to me, facing a high glass showcase piled with trays of cakes. I saw him reach up and take one. He put it into his pocket. He reached up for another, and put this one into his mouth.

I looked around wondering why nobody noticed

what he was doing. A woman directly behind the counter near him had her head down arranging some trays and wasn't paying him any attention. She didn't act as if she knew I was alive, either. The Dummy hadn't even finished the cake in his mouth before he had reached up, grabbed another, and stuffed that one in, too.

I had to envy him. If there was any way not to break into an allowance he had the secret. To make sure he didn't forget how, he did it again. Two more cakes. Zip zip. One into his mouth, the other into his pocket.

He wasn't the least bit crafty about it. He simply reached up and took what he wanted. The woman behind the counter must have been blind not to notice, I thought, and then she came over toward me wiping her hands on her apron, giving me a tired smile.

"Yes?"

The glass showcase in front of me ran lengthwise across the store to join the one the Dummy was raiding. I looked down at a tray full of jelly doughnuts. Surrounding it were other trays of different cakes and cookies, but jelly doughnuts are what make my mouth water.

While I stood there getting weak in the knees about which ones I wanted the most, I saw the Dummy out of the corner of my eye reach for some more cakes and knock some off the top. They landed on the floor where the custard and the powdered sugar topping mixed into a mess. That didn't bother him. He scooped it up, his mouth opened and into it he pushed some of the stuff from the floor. The rest went into his pocket. What a gooey mess he must have in there!

While this nut was robbing her blind and eating his way through the store the bakery woman was more worried over what I wanted.

"Yes?" she asked again.

I put my finger on the glass. "That jelly doughnut there—how much is it?"

The Dummy heard me. He came over and touched my shoulder, still wearing that wide goofy smile.

"Aaaah!" he said.

"Hi," I said. I kept my finger on the glass not wanting to lose my pinpointing of the jelly doughnut with the most appeal. "That one," I told the woman. "Third one from the end, two rows down."

She slid the back of the case open and as she reached inside the Dummy tapped my arm. When he saw he had my attention, he stuck his hand into his pocket. It came out holding a crushed cake, its creamy yellow filling mixed with vanilla frosting and some melted chocolate. It looked awful.

"Aaaah," he said smiling, bobbing his head, pushing the goo closer to my face.

I shook my head.

"No, thanks." I pointed to the glass case in front of me. "I've got that big jelly doughnut coming."

He pulled his gift offering back and craned his head to look down at the doughnut tray inside. Nodding, he straightened up and tapped my arm again, pointing toward the rear opening of the store behind the glass counters.

"My . . ." he said. "My . . ."

I waited, but that was all he said. So I turned away to make sure the woman picked out the doughnut I wanted. She showed it to me wrapped in a thin piece of paper.

"That's it," I said. Then, "How much is it?"

"Eight cents. Two for fifteen."

The Dummy was shoving another messy cake in my face. I drew back, shaking my head, saying, "No, thanks," and finally had to duck to avoid it. "Okay, make it two," I told the woman behind the counter, recklessly.

She put them in a bag. I paid her and she rang up the sale.

The Dummy broke into a big smile. "Dong?" he asked me.

I stared at him, puzzled, then realized he was talking about the sound the cash register made.

"Yeah. I guess so," I said, feeling kind of silly.

The Dummy pointed to the rear opening of the store again. "My . . ." he said.

What did he mean? I saw him reach for another cake and start cramming it into his mouth. I looked at the woman. She had turned her back and started sweeping behind the counter. I didn't have any more time to waste; those jelly doughnuts in the bag felt too inviting. So I waved goodby to the Dummy and started out.

"Aaaah!" he said smiling.

"Aaaah yourself," I said, and went out the door.

I ate one doughnut on the way home. There I gave the other one to Susie, noticing right away that with all my experience, I'd eaten the wrong one. Hers had the most jelly inside. She grinned, licking her fingers.

"How come you got two? Did you get your allowance?"

"This dumb bakery," I said. "I could've got them for nothing. Plus a lot of great big gooey ones."

She knows how cheap I am usually. "How come?"

I told her about the Dummy.

"Oh, him," she said. "He wasn't stealing exactly. His mother is the baker there. She works in the back where you can't see her."

I remember him pointing there and saying "My . . . my . . . ."

"You mean you know him?"

She licked some more jelly off her fingers. "Sure. Everybody does. He's a new boy. His name is Alan Harper. Why do you call him Dummy?"

I told her about the incident with the football and then about finding him in the middle of the street traffic. "Plus all that 'Aaaah' stuff," I said. "That's all he ever says."

Susie nodded. "That's because he's retarded. He's in my class."

"Your class?" I repeated, surprised. "But he's older than I am, I bet."

She nodded again. "Sure. He's there because he's re-tarded, you dummy."

"What do you mean—retarded?"

She tapped her head. "There's something wrong up here."

I should have known, I guess, when he just lay there and bleated that "Aaaah" after I slapped him. It was too late but now I wished I hadn't done that.

Oh . . . very nicewarm . . . light . . . sun up there . . .
look at . . . white . . . things. Up-in-sky-things.
Soft   see-through things   blow high
Horse.   Horses.   Face.   More face.
Big round bump face   Ah . . . . . .

This place.   Inside big-wall-window-place . . .
walk busy-bump-look-girls   boys   people.
So many things   people   Hurry walk fast . . .
Books.
Sit-open books-look up   no talk   no-no-talk-
                                    only-sit-look.

Listen . . .
Talk   talk   talk.   What-is what is?
Oh look window . . . Fly bird. More fly bird.
Funny   fly bird.
Oh mad-look teacher.   No look bird
no-look-bird-things-out . . . only teacher . . .
look-sit-listen-no more look out hear-hear-hear.
Only   Only
Why no look pretty fly bird things only sit-look-listen?

4

Mr. Alvarado is a Chicano, part of our minority Mexican-American group here in Bellwood, Los Angeles County. He's our English teacher. He happens to be a very good teacher, and knows exactly what he wants. Mostly, he wants us to learn to express ourselves. Communication, he says, is our only hope and without that we're nowhere. It's not hard to believe Mr. Alvarado. He communicates just fine.

Every week we're given a topic to write about, and read aloud in class. None of us are great writers or have anything important to say, but Mr. Alvarado doesn't mind. He says the main idea is to get our brains accustomed to observing and thinking, and then telling about it.

The subject this week was about people we had met and found interesting. I couldn't think of anybody else so I wrote about the Dummy.

My turn came to stand up and read. The first time I mentioned the name Dummy a few guys snickered. As I went on more and more of the class started laughing until finally everybody was roaring, stamping feet, laughing so hard and so loud I could hardly hear my own words.

All I'd done was write about how we met and so on. I didn't think it was so funny, but the waves of laughter bouncing off the walls got to me and before I finished reading I was grinning like everybody else. Some kids sat doubled over, holding their sides, and girls were wiping tears off their eyes from laughing. There was a lot of clapping. Everybody's face seemed split into a wide smile.

I felt the room quieting down and glanced at Mr. Alvarado leaning in front of his desk. He wasn't smiling. His arms were crossed over his chest. His face was grim, set in hard lines, his black eyes glittering. He waited patiently until the laughter died down, and the coughing spasms and foot stamping subsided.

"Is that all, Comstock?" he asked softly. "Are you finished?"

I had a terrible sinking feeling in my stomach. Something was wrong. I looked down at the pages in my notebook.

"Yes, sir. That's it."

"Be seated," he said curtly.

I flopped down fast, feeling suddenly very warm. He looked at me without expression, then surveyed the rest of the class, his eyes flicking from one seat to another. Normally, he's a very good-natured man. I could recognize the change right away.

"Congratulations, Comstock," he said. His eyes lifted to the others. "You are all to be congratulated—for your total lack of humanity and understanding."

There were nervous coughs from behind me. I felt hot, my ears burning, and I sank back in my seat, keeping eyes on Mr. Alvarado. There wasn't any place to go and hide.

Mr. Alvarado's swarthy color had lightened. His eyes touched me again, then flicked away to stare bleakly at the others. I could feel the contempt in his voice now, a low growling note.

"I was never before aware that there was the slightest thing funny about being retarded," he said. "Maybe I've been missing something." His eyes returned to me. "Is your subject brain-damaged?"

I shrugged. My voice sounded weak. "I don't know."

He nodded curtly. "You don't know," he said. He rubbed the dark stubble of his chin. "It doesn't make too much difference, really. One such state is as helpless as the other. If you'll laugh at one, you'll find the other equally amusing."

I cleared my throat. "I didn't mean it to be funny. I only wrote about it. I mean, like that's the way it was."

His glance was gloomy, his voice sharp and unforgiving.

"Did you ever stop to wonder how small town politicians and demogogues manage to hold and influence their audiences?"

I shook my head dumbly. It wasn't anything I'd ever done any thinking about.

"They use the same tactics," he continued. "They hold up to ridicule what neither they nor their audience can understand. The level of intelligence in most rural areas is low, to begin with, so they have no problem at all manipulating their listeners. I'd hoped we could do better here."

"Yes, sir," I mumbled.

I felt everybody's eyes on my back, and knew they'd never forgive me for sucking them all into this.

Mr. Alvarado's hard eyes levelled at me again.

"You did your assignment but I can't let it pass. You got your laughs cheap at the expense of an unfortunate and innocent victim."

Feet shuffled behind me and there were nervous uncomfortable coughs. Nobody was prepared for this side of Mr. Alvarado.

"All of you were equally at fault," he said, "for letting yourselves be taken in. A certain amount of courage is needed to resist mass opinion. But we're supposed to have made some progress since the last lynching. Being mentally retarded means being crippled, in a sense. I'm willing to listen if anybody cares to explain what's funny about being a cripple. Anybody?"

He waited but nobody volunteered. The room got very quiet. Mr. Alvarado nodded.

"All right, Comstock. It was a mistake and we all have to live or fall with our thoughts. If you want a mark you'll have to try again. Perhaps next time you'll be able to come up with something better suited to your assignment. Our topic was contact with another person. By contact, I mean understanding . . . Any questions?" He waited again. Then he turned away. "Class dismissed."

I pushed myself out of my chair, picked up my books, and got out of there fast.

Oh bad very bad.
Hat   My . . .   Mine . . .   My red hat.
Boys   Girls   Many boys-girls.   Take hat.
Push   pull   hit   run my hat
         run   fall   not find hat.
Too many push-pull-hit . . . . . . fall-run my hat.

One.   One-boy.   This boy.
Friend.   My funny   what-throwkick-hit-friend.
Get hat.   My red hat.
Walk walk walk . . . . . .
Things.   Nice things.   Br . . r . . rr fly bird.
More things.
More walk-walk with my one-boy
House   My . . .   mine . . . My house.

No more one-boy.

5

On my way home from school, I heard yelling and cheering around the corner, like a big game was in progress.

When I got there I could see why everybody sounded so happy. They were playing the game where you drive somebody crazy. I'm not sure this game has a name, but everybody knows what it is. It could be called Grab-your-hat, for example.

Here's how it works. Somebody grabs something of yours. If that happens to be your hat, then that's it. The idea of the game is for you to try to get your hat back from whoever has it. He passes it over your head, or to the person nearest him, or anybody available who can catch it out of your reach. You run back and forth, trying to guess which way it's going, jumping,

32

trying to get it before somebody else does. If you accomplish that, then you've won and it's somebody else's turn to chase back and forth and be frustrated. I suppose the first big bully who grabbed a smaller kid's hat started the whole dumb game.

There were a lot of kids spread out in a big circle. When I saw who was in the middle, chasing back and forth, I could understand why they were all having such a good time.

They had the Dummy's hat, a funny kind of floppy red baseball cap with a long bill. The kid who had it held it up. The Dummy charged. Somebody stuck his foot out and tripped him. He fell, and everybody laughed. When he got up and went after his hat again, the kid who had it waited till the Dummy was almost on top of him before passing it off to the fellow next to him.

"Aaaah!" the Dummy said.

That's the way it went, over and over again, until I got sick watching. The Dummy was too slow and clumsy, he didn't have the right reflexes, he couldn't move right when he had to. It was pathetic. He would make a rush for his cap, eyes and mouth wide open, his hands outstretched, making that awful "aaaah" sound. They'd trip him, let him get up, fool him, trip him again, allow him to get close, almost touch the cap, and then—off it would go to somebody else.

He was sucking wind, his chest heaving, tears of frustration streaking his face. He didn't get angry. Maybe he didn't know how.

33

I couldn't stand it any longer. The next time the hat was flipped I was able to reach up and grab it. Everybody cheered. They thought they had another soldier. "That's all," I said. "He's had enough. Give somebody else a chance to go crazy."

I walked out of the circle and they began to yell and yammer, crowding up close, their faces mean and angry, asking me what the idea was. I had to push a few of them away.

"Can't you tell he's a sick kid?" I said. "Come on— you've had your fun."

I beckoned to the Dummy. "It's okay. I got it," and showed him the hat.

He smiled through the tears. "Aaaah!" he said. His arms went up, hands outstretched.

"Yeah. Sure. We got it. Come on."

He walked toward me, his eyes fixed on his red cap like it was a magnet. Somebody booted him from behind and then shoved him forward, knocking him off-balance right into me. I managed to keep us both from falling.

I put his cap back on his head and looked directly at the kid who had knocked him forward. He glared at me for a second, then backed up. I was mad enough to hit him, and I guess I showed it. He stepped out of the way as I came through. So did a few others. I walked right up to them like I never intended to stop, pulling the Dummy along behind me by one arm. His hand felt hot and heavy. There were a lot of dumb remarks as we passed through but we kept going and I didn't look back. When we were clear, I turned to the Dummy.

"Come on. I'll take you home. Where do you live?"

A slight frown passed over his face. He thought about it a while. One arm suddenly shot up.

"My . . . my . . . " he said.

"Okay," I said. "Lead the way."

It wasn't very far but it took a long time to get there. Almost everything that caught the Dummy's eye interested him and he would stop to look it over. He was like a bee buzzing from flower to flower sipping the nectar.

The first thing that interested him was a fire hydrant. He looked it over from all sides, squatting to peer at it. Walking all around it, touching it.

"Nice," he said. "Nice . . . thing."

I never thought before about a fire hydrant being nice.

"Yeah," I said. "It's okay."

He touched it again. "I . . . I . . . " he said.

"It's iron, I guess."

That wasn't what he meant. He touched his cap.

"My . . . my . . . "

I got it.

"That's right," I said. "They're both the same color. Red."

He beamed. He took his cap off and looked at it lovingly.

35

"My," he said. "My red."

"It's a hat," I said hastily. "Or maybe you can call it a cap. A red hat or a red cap."

"Aaaah," he said. He put it back on his head and touched it proudly. "My...red...huh...huh...hat."

I nodded. My face felt red, too.

"Yeah," I said.

He turned to look back to the direction we'd come from. He touched his hat again.

"You . . . you," he said.

"It's okay," I said.

We were having a real conversation.

He liked a telephone pole next. Just an ordinary telephone pole, the wood splintered or gouged out where some kids had cut their initials. He put his hand on the pole.

"Woo," he said. "Woo. Woo."

He leaned against the wood, hugging the pole. He looked up, smiled and pointed. A blue jay was sitting on a wire at the top.

"Brrr," the Dummy said, waving his arms.

I nodded.

He surprised me then by whistling. It was a beautiful trilling whistle, sharp and clear. A bird call.

"Hey, that's pretty good," I said.

The little bird high on the wire cocked its head. It bent down and trilled its own reply. The Dummy smiled.

"Brrr," he said.

I tapped his arm. "We were going home, remember? Let's go."

We were moving again but it didn't last long. After a few more steps he was peering down at a stain on the sidewalk. Rain and weather had done something to the cement, and people walking on it, and passing traffic. I noticed it was very much like a painting. Cloud-like effects separated by tiny pebbles and some streaks of tar stains. The more I looked at it, the more interesting it became. I walked around the square indentations framing the picture, from all angles. I never noticed before how interesting a dirty street sidewalk could be.

Suddenly I realized the Dummy had moved on. Now he was staring down at a chip in the cement curb. I looked at that, too, but it didn't seem to me to be anything more than just a chipped curb. The Dummy passed on to examine a wall next to a vacant lot. It had bits of paper poster stuck on it, green stains, a lot of holes and scars on the bricks. It looked like a dirty old wall but, after my first annoyed glance, I saw it had the same effect on me the sidewalk had. This was like a modern painting, too, the stains and blotches and scraps of faded paper somehow making a very interesting design.

I could tell by now that, at the rate we were going, it would take about a week to walk the Dummy home. He liked to look at fences, garbage cans, thrown scraps, pieces of paper the wind had blown along the street, old cans, bottles, discarded cigarette and cigar butts, a lot of crummy things. After a while, I felt I was looking at the world through a microscope.

"Nice," he would say every once in a while. "Things."

I never dreamed I'd be agreeing with him. But by the time I got the Dummy home, I had discovered there was a whole new world inside the world I took for granted. Something had been added to the original by time or accident, making everything more interesting than before. Sometimes, if you looked closely enough, you saw it was even beautiful.

I sort of wondered who was the real Dummy, after all.

I   *Me*   *Mine*
Red.   *My red . . .*   *My red hat.*   *Head.*
For head. . .

Walk.   *Walk . . .*
Look things my number-one-hit-throwkick-funny-what-boy.

House.   *My . . .*   *In.*
Look boy in house.

Number-one-boy go.   *Away . . .go.*
Why go away?

6

"I hear you're going to get beat up," Susie said, "for putting your two cents in over Alan Harper." The news must have got around fast. "Why did you do it, Neil?"

I didn't know the answer myself. I had played that same dumb game maybe a thousand times in my life, either with a bunch of kids grabbing my hat or book, or me doing the same to them. It never seemed like any big deal before and nobody ever became hysterical about it. Once in a while you would run into a crybaby, of course, but usually that was a little kid.

"He's such a meatball," I said. "He can't move. He didn't have a chance. They could keep him running for a million years and he'd never be able to get his hat. That's why."

40

There wasn't any question about him really being a Dummy. He couldn't say the simplest words. He just seemed to be able to walk and look at things and smile and eat.

"Where did you go with him?"

"I took him home. That's all."

"Did you meet his sister?"

"Is that who she was?"

The Dummy lived a few blocks away from the bakery in an old one-story wooden house, stained and dirty, with grass growing high and wild all around it. The windows had been broken and the panes replaced with cardboard or pieces of wood. If ever a house looked small and miserable and rotten, this one did.

On the walk home, although it hadn't seemed possible, the Dummy finally ran out of things to look at, or maybe he remembered I was trying to get him home.

"My . . . my . . . " he said suddenly and started to dogtrot down the street.

We were approaching the bakery and I thought that was why he looked so happy—going to try his luck again with all those gooey cakes. But he ran past it another block, then stopped short in front of a house set back off the street behind high grass.

Somebody was sitting hunched over on the long wooden slats of the porch. A young girl, her elbows on her knees, her hands cupping her face, stared past us into space. She was thin, with long black uncombed hair, and bare-legged, her dress short and dirty, her arms and legs smeared too. She stared into the distance even when the Dummy stopped in front of her and waved his arms.

"My . . . my . . . " he said, bobbing his head to indicate the girl.

"I brought him home," I told her. "Some kids at school were giving him a hard time."

She took no notice of either of us and I had the strange feeling that she didn't even know she was there herself. The way her smoky-blue eyes were staring out into space she could have been a million miles away. I couldn't blame her, because if she looked around her all she would have seen was a lot of grass, dirt and garbage cans.

I just couldn't believe that house.

"Do you live here?" I asked the Dummy.

He bobbed his head five or six times, rapidly.

"In . . . in . . . inside . . . house."

"Her, too?" I asked.

He smiled his special goofy grin. His finger jabbed out toward the girl. He tapped his chest.

"My . . . my . . . "

"Your sister? Is she your sister?"

You couldn't be sure from what he said. Her reaction was zero zero. She stayed sitting where she was, hunched up, cradling her arms, staring toward Timbuctoo. They didn't look much like brother or sister. The Dummy was good-sized, fairhaired and chunky, with blue eyes and ruddy complexion. Actually he was a nice-looking kid and, if you'd never heard him say "Aaaah" and smile, you might think he was normal. The girl, I noticed now, was a little older by a year or two, with sallow skin, her eyes big and so dark they looked black. She was even pretty in a wild sort of way. Maybe fierce-looking would be better. Her nose was thin and delicate, her lips firm and set.

The Dummy was tugging at my sleeve. He pointed toward the door.

"Come look my," he said.

"Okay. I'll take a quick look," I said, "but I got to be getting home. It's late." He looked blank and I tapped my wrist watch. "Late," I said. I made a big circle in the air. It didn't help any. "Tick-tick late," I added stubbornly.

His eyebrows shot up and he smiled, repeating, "Tick tick late."

I looked at him closely. There wasn't any comprehension at all in his eyes. He was merely saying the words. It gave me a weird feeling. Talking without knowing what you were saying just didn't seem human.

I shrugged and followed him past the girl up the dirty rickety steps. He stopped when his hand touched the doorknob and smiled.

"This . . . door."

It was dark inside. Cardboards and boards aren't any substitute for windows. The house was small, cluttered with odds and ends of furniture, and clothing strewn all over chairs, hanging on doors. I bumped into a lot of things and my nose didn't like the dank smell. The

43

room was such a mess I didn't have the heart to look at the kitchen. Whoever took care of the place wouldn't have won any medals from Good Housekeeping.

The Dummy had my arm. He waved one of his.

"My . . . my . . . "

I figured that some day I'd have the time and patience to wait until he found the next word. But I wasn't ready for that yet. Meanwhile I operated by guesswork.

Next the Dummy showed me a bedroom. It was dark and messy, too. Neither of its two small beds had been made. I didn't see a mirror or a bookcase or a dresser, only clothing heaped on the floor.

"This your bedroom?" I asked.

His head bobbed, smiling. He put his hands together and placed them under his chin.

"Sleep," he said. "Bed . . . room. Zzz . . . zzz . . . zzz."

"Does she sleep here, too?" Because his expression remained blank I waved my arm like he did. "The girl . . . outside." I made myself hunch up and look thin and withdrawn, trying to capture her expression.

The Dummy laughed and clapped his hands. "Des . . . Des . . . " I had to wait for the rest. He took a deep breath and all of a sudden he had it. "Des . . .de . . . mo . . . na."

"Desdemona?" I'd heard that name somewhere before. "Is she your sister or what?"

He pointed to one of the beds. "My . . . my . . . "

"Okay," I muttered. "What's the difference? Well, I

44

got to be going now." I wanted to ask him his name and tell him mine, but for some dumb reason I felt tongue-tied or self-conscious. So I pointed to his hat. "Take care of your hat now. Watch out for those kids."

He seemed to understand. He took it off his head and extended it to me.

"My . . ." he said. "My . . . red . . ."

I nodded. "That's right. Say, do you have a father?"

He looked at me not understanding. I started to make hand motions and then realized I couldn't pantomime the word. I rubbed my jaw and backed off a step. He did the same.

"Fa . . . fa . . . fa . . . ?"

"Forget it." I tapped my wristwatch. "I got to be going now. Thanks for showing me the place. So long."

I started for the door and he understood I was leaving. A look of disappointment flashed across his face.

"Way . . . way," he cried. He ran across the living room, bumping into a lot of furniture, until he reached a small table near the wall. He opened a drawer and took out something, which he handed to me, breathing hard and looking very pleased and excited. It was one of those gooey cakes I'd seen him grab at the bakery.

"Eat," he said, rubbing his stomach. He opened his mouth, showed his teeth and made loud chomping noises. "Eat."

It was in my hand before I realized what a good host he was. I couldn't tell him it was too gooey a mess. Outside, I blinked and took a deep breath, like coming

45

out of a cave. The girl he called Desdemona was gone.

When I was far enough away I fed the Dummy's cake to some birds. They didn't complain about its sogginess or ask how long it had been in his drawer, or if it wasn't spoiled by now, or had germs. They even fought over the crumbs.

Now Susie, who seemed to know about everything, was telling me the girl was the Dummy's sister.

"Is she retarded—like he is?" I asked her.

She shrugged. "I don't think so, but she won't talk."

"Won't or can't?"

"What's the difference?"

Later, when I went to bed, I looked in Susie's room, found her sitting up in bed, reading and eating an apple.

"Goodnight," I said. She looked at me as if I'd suddenly blown my mind. I couldn't blame her. I hadn't wished her goodnight in years. "I think the Dummy and his sister sleep in the same bedroom."

Susie nodded without losing her place on either the book or the apple.

"Of course, you dope," she said. "They're very poor."

It took me a long time to go to sleep.

Talk   *things . . . Hello how are you?*
Walk   *people.*   *Hello how are you?*
How are you?

Store   *my*   *nice*
Eat   *eat*
No more hello how are you.

7

I tried hard to forget the Dummy, to get him out of my mind, but it wasn't easy. Knowing him was like dropping a stone into still water, spreading ripples in ever widening circles. They reached out and caught you eventually.

I was caught too, by his scarecrow sister Desdemona. First I found out why her name was familiar. She was a famous character in the play *Othello* written by William Shakespeare. Othello's wife. A creep named Iago got Othello jealous and he smothered her to death. It's a real wild and hairy story. I wondered if the Dummy's sister knew she was named after a famous dead girl.

I could still see her in my mind, sitting silently, dirty, scrawny, hunched up and hugging herself with her thin arms, searching the horizon. She was like a castaway looking far out at the same spot maybe a hundred times, despairing and desperate, afraid to yell, "Help," any more.

Was she so detached, not part of anything, because she had a retarded kid brother who acted half his age? Would it have helped if maybe somebody had explained to her that he was sick and couldn't help it? Maybe then she might have talked, not stared right through you as if you weren't there.

I couldn't decide which was worse—not talking, or talking and sounding like a moron. There was more to it than being poor and living in a dark crummy old house that was falling apart. If it cost too much to fix up windows, you could put in electric lights or maybe even kerosene lamps or candles. You didn't have to throw clothes on the floor and not sweep or clean up and live like some kind of animal. It got me kind of steamed up just thinking about it.

I decided there were worse things than being poor. Not being able to talk or say what you wanted to say, for instance. Not to be able to even think of what you wanted to say. That was another. Nor to understand what people were saying to you. Being helpless when they teased or took advantage of you. Feeling dumb and stupid and unable to do anything about it. Feeling not wanted or even liked.

I remembered his goofy smile. Maybe it didn't make

49

any difference to him. Was it possible he didn't feel or think anything? That was like being a vegetable. I got up a good sweat just thinking about that.

I closed my eyes and pretended to be the Dummy. In less than five seconds flat I was so frightened I had to open them. It was too scary to feel that helpless, at everybody's mercy. The only way to manage was not to feel or care. About anthing. That way, you could get by. I wondered if that was the Dummy's secret. No brains, no feelings. Was that it?

I remembered what Susie had told me about the Dummy's mother working for the bakery. What was she like? I knew one thing for certain; she didn't know or care much about keeping house.

I went back to the bakery to try to see the Dummy's mother, determined not to let myself get hypnotized by the jelly doughnuts and blow my mind. The woman behind the counter was very patient and let me take my time. I pretended to look over all the cakes on display. A nice warm smell of baking bread came from the back room. I heard a lot of noise, pots being banged around, metal clanking, but I couldn't see her. Finally I gave up and bought some jelly doughnuts.

Susie caught on this time I gave her the extra one.

"I love jelly doughnuts," she said, her mouth full, "but you're wasting your time as well as your money."

I tried to look innocent. "What?"

She licked jelly off from between her fingers. "Alan Harper's mother, the baker there, doesn't talk much better than he does. I think there's some kind of curse on that family."

"How do you mean?"

"The father is supposed to be in jail. Or maybe it's an insane asylum. He's supposed to be crazy. He either killed somebody or just flipped his wig. Anyway, he's locked up for keeps."

"How do you know that?"

Susie took her ear lobe and stretched it between her thumb and forefinger. "I heard."

I stared at her. "But how do you know it's true?"

"I don't," she said. "But it fits, all right."

I was puzzled. "If nobody in the family talks, how could anybody outside know? Maybe whoever gave you the story made it all up."

"Why would they go to the trouble of doing that?" she asked.

"I don't know. Sometimes people do. Unless maybe his sister told somebody."

Susie laughed. "Desdemona? She doesn't talk to anybody. Not even me. And, you know, everybody talks to me."

"Then how do you know she's no dummy, too, like he is?"

"She gets good marks in school. Without even trying. That's how," Susie said.

I kept watching for the Dummy's sister and finally saw her at an outdoor recess. The other girls in their shorts, blouses and sneakers were playing games, running, laughing, screaming the way girls do when they're playing. Desdemona sat apart, like she couldn't care less what they were doing, her hands folded over her knees, her gaze as far away as the last time, like she was waiting for a particular cloud to form over the horizon. She didn't look as ratty as the other time. Her face and legs looked cleaner and her long black hair was combed and not so wild-looking. But instead of wearing socks and sneakers like the other girls she was barefoot.

There was a scream from one of the girls and the ball they were throwing around bounced and stopped near Desdemona, a large white volley ball. She ignored it. The girl who had missed catching it came running up, her arms extended, hands apart, to stop and say something I couldn't hear. Was she asking the Dummy's sister to throw the ball to her? Desdemona just kept looking off into the distance as if she hadn't heard. The other girl, looking annoyed, came and scooped the ball up, her lip curled and muttering something under her breath. Judging from her expression, it was something sarcastic. The Dummy's sister continued to sit hunched up, staring out into space. The girl walked away with the volley ball, tossing her long blonde hair angrily.

"Forget it, Carol," another girl called. "You're just wasting your breath. You know what she's like."

The girl called Carol threw the ball then and they all ran after it, laughing and screaming again. I sneaked another look at the Dummy's sister. She continued to sit there unmoved, wrapped up in her own world. You couldn't tell from her expression whether she even noticed they were gone.

I wanted to go over and say hello but she seemed so aloof I didn't dare. I just kept staring trying to get up the courage. Her head turned slowly. Her eyes, like a fixed beacon, swept past me without a sign of recognition, without the slightest change of expression. A moment later her head turned away to once more face the distant horizon.

I got the message. *Don't hear anything. Don't see anybody. Leave me alone, you cats. Get lost.*

Maybe that was the way you had to be in her situation. It wasn't exactly my idea of living, but then my old man's not in jail or a loony bin. I don't have a mother who runs a sloppy house or a kid brother who's an idiot. Maybe Susie was right and there was a curse on the family. It would be a heck of a thing to have to live with.

On my way home, strictly on a hunch, I tried the bakery again. I wanted to see the Dummy's mother but, so as not to lose another battle of willpower to those jelly doughnuts, this time I stayed outside and looked in. All I could see was the woman who waited on me, in her usual place behind the counter checking out the cash register.

The sound of some cans banging came from the alley alongside the bakery. So there must be a side entrance. I headed around the corner, feeling the heat of the oven and smelling fresh bread more clearly with every step. The brick wall was hot to my touch. As I came closer to the side entrance, a woman stepped out carrying a large wide tray. She lifted the lid off one of several big garbage cans and started scraping dough into it.

She looked very old and gray. Then I noticed her hands and face were dusted white with flour, which gave her that weird pasty look. Her hair was black streaked with gray, or maybe it was more flour. Her sleeves were rolled up, her arms very white. She was sweating.

"How's Alan?" I asked.

She continued scraping away a big ladlefull of dough from the tray. Hadn't she heard me? A thin frowning line formed between her eyes and she stopped what she was doing and looked at me like she hadn't noticed me there before, her eyes dull and very tired.

"Alan," I said again. "How's he doing?"

She shook her head as if puzzled and wiped her hands on her soiled white apron. She pushed some loose hair back from over her eyes. Her lips worked silently and then she tilted her head and looked at me out of the corner of her eyes, a strange look, sly and cunning. It kind of scared me.

"What you want?" she asked finally, her voice flat and too loud. Nasal. Sounding like a horn.

I shrugged. "I just asked how your son was."

She wiped her hands again, brushed more hair out of

her eyes, and gave me that tilted corner look again. "You know him?"

"Sure," I said smiling and trying to act pleasant and sociable. "We go to the same school."

Her lips twisted, she took a deep breath and exhaled noisily. It was almost a sigh.

"Trouble," she said. "Is always trouble. Very busy now. Goodbye."

She banged her tray against the can, tearing the rest of the sticky dough loose with her hands. She slammed back the lid of the can, tucked the wide tray under her arm and headed for the open door.

"Trouble," she was muttering under her breath. "Is always more trouble."

She disappeared inside, leaving me alone in the alley with the garbage cans. I kicked one of them hard. It hurt my toe some but it was worth it.

Oh bad very bad boys
Hit   Hit   Hurt.   Why?
Laugh game   Push-turn-laugh game.

My boy.   My number one hit-throwkick-my-funny-
what-honk-honk-cross-street-red-what-my-red-what
boy . . .
Friend.
Oh no look   All hit my number one . . . . . .
Not nice   stop-stop   oh bad . . .
Run away. No look bad-hit-my number one . . . Hurt.
Red   red on face   on on nose mouth red-red-what?
Blood what.
Go away   no good   in   in   hurt   in.

Oh very bad day   this one.
No hello-how-are-you-day.

8

The next time I saw the Dummy it hurt in more ways than one. Some people carry grudges and have to get even. I'd forgotten a simple little thing like that.

It was after school again and leaving the yard I heard yells and laughter. Then I heard that strange bleating sound, "Aaaah!" and I knew they had him again.

This time they were roughing him up on purpose, not using his funny red hat as an excuse. They were pushing him back and forth, spinning him, shoving him from behind, knocking him all around the circle.

When I came over I saw there were bigger kids in the circle of morons now, some my age and older. One glance at their faces when they saw me made it clear this was the way they had planned it: use the Dummy as bait, having their fun with him, but get me. I suppose they felt they had to teach me a lesson about butting in when I wasn't wanted and spoiling their sport.

It didn't take too long before they had me down and all I could do was take it and hope they got tired soon. They pushed my face into the ground and all that stuff and then it was all over.

I lay there until it got quiet. Then I sat up to wipe my bloody nose and lips. My hands were covered with dirt and bloody too, like my face was, and shaking so I could hardly hold my handkerchief.

I got up feeling awfully tired and aching all over, and after one step decided to wait until the world settled down. Then I saw the Dummy standing about twenty yards away, his back against a wall, looking very scared and white-faced. His red hat was in his hands and he kept squeezing it. His lips moved but he didn't say anything.

I didn't feel much like talking. My lips were puffy and bruised and a couple of teeth loose. I just slapped some dirt off my pants, waved to him and started home, all my muscles and bones creaking and complaining, feeling about a hundred years old. I had to rest a while and then it got better. Floating along, I had the feeling I was being followed. At first when I turned around I couldn't see a thing. Then my vision cleared and I saw him. He was facing me, standing stock still about half a block away. All I could really see clearly was his red hat on his white face.

59

After awhile I looked around again and there he was, still a half block away. He didn't try to come any closer but kept following me at the same pace.

When I reached my house, I turned once more. There he was. I waited a moment to see if he would come closer but he didn't. Finally I knew I had to go upstairs. I waved but he didn't wave back. He just stood there silently, like a white-faced ghost with a red hat.

I caught heck, of course, for fighting and getting my clothes ruined but I was too tired to make any excuses. I was even too tired to eat dinner which came as a big surprise to my folks. I went to sleep early and dreamed I had a shot at every one of those kids, one at a time. I did a whole lot better in the dream, and it was more fun. Susie saved what was left of those kids by waking me up.

"I thought you were supposed to be a good fighter," she said.

"So did I," I said.

"How many of them were there?"

"I didn't count."

"Boy, you sure are a mess."

"Is that what you woke me up to tell me?"

She shook her head. "Was it because of—of—him?" She hated to use the word Dummy.

"What's the difference?" I said.

"Are you going to get even, Neil?"

It hurt to smile. "I was just doing that—until you woke me up."

"I mean, in real life, you dope. Are you going to get even?"

I thought about it. Finally I said, "I don't know. I'll see how it works out."

"You better not," she said. "You're liable to hurt somebody."

I looked at her. "Well, I don't feel as if anybody's been kissing me, either."

"You know what I mean, Neil. You might do worse than that. You know what a temper you have."

"Yeah," I said bitterly. "I sure better watch that terrible temper of mine. Next time I'm liable to kill myself."

She shook her head. Then she raised her arm and I felt something cool against my cheek.

"What's that?"

"Lemonade, you dope. I made you some lemonade."

I sat up and looked at it. She'd even put a straw in the glass.

"What did you do that for?" I asked.

"Because you're such a dope, you dope."

Then she said goodnight, leaned over fast, kissed me on the cheek and ran out of the room. I couldn't remember her doing that since she was a little baby.

The cold lemonade hurt my teeth but it was good.

Hello how are you?   *Hello how are you?*
How are you   *are you?*
Walk . . . . . .   *Things.*
More walk . . . . . .

Ah   *nice*   *Eat eat . . .*
Oh   *what?*
Mad face.   *What?*

Ah My number one hit-kick-honkhonk-red-what boy

Thing   *My thing.*   *More red . . .*
Boom Boom.   *Ratatat tat*   *More ratatat tat.*
My ratatat.   *Boom boom*
Boomboomboomboomboom.

9

My pop is a toy salesman. He represents a few manufacturers and goes to different stores trying to sell their toys, lugging around a big sample case containing whatever line he's trying to unload. As a rule, his route covers only the city, but sometimes he has to travel to try and sell some out-of-town store-buyer. He gripes a lot about that but he must make a pretty good living because we seem to eat and pay the rent regularly. He sells everything: Baby dolls that wet themselves or cry, toy bazookas which fire shells that smoke, a lot of novelty games, puzzles, and so on. Sometimes he has a sample that gets worn-out showing it around, and then he brings it home and gives it to us kids.

He called me over now and opened his big suitcase.

"Maybe you're too old for this but the firm is discontinuing the line, so you can have it. We used to get ten bucks for it."

It was a toy drum, the metal sides painted a bright red, with little white wooden drumsticks and a leather strap to hang around your neck while you beat it. I remembered having one like it when I was a little kid. I'd broken it soon afterward and never got another—a lesson, that money didn't grow on trees and you were supposed to take care of your things and not break them.

The one my pop was showing me now was practically perfect, so new you had to look closely at the drumhead to notice the skin was slightly soiled. Apart from that it was swell, with a good sound. I figured this might give the Dummy something to be happy about for a change.

It was Saturday, a good day for a present. I put the drum in a paper bag, so it would be a surprise.

It was a cold and cloudy morning, not too many people out. The Dummy's sister happened to be one of them, sitting on the wooden front steps of their house in her usual position, thin arms clasped about her legs, hunched over, staring out into space. She was wearing a short thin dress. Her feet were bare and looked as if they'd been covering a lot of ground. I came up the walk and stopped in front of her. She didn't bat an eye.

"Hi," I said conversationally. "Aren't you cold?"

I decided I must have been talking to myself. Another step forward took me close enough to touch her.

If she didn't notice me now there was something wrong with her sight as well as her hearing.

"Is your brother home?"

Her eyes shifted slightly and for a second I thought there was a glimmer of recognition, but it was gone before I could be sure. She didn't speak but her fierce expression changed. The eyes that had seemed black now became a dark smokey-blue, and her face softened to a look of curiosity. I had the impression she was wondering what kind of a nut I was, what was I doing there, and didn't I have anything better to do than stand like a lump trying to strike up a conversation with somebody who wasn't interested? Her stare was so unyielding it made me uncomfortable, like I was trespassing in somebody's private garden.

What would happen if I sat down alongside her? I was afraid to try it. Instead, I tapped the drumskin inside the paper bag. It made a <u>thump</u> sound which she gave no indication of hearing.

"It's for your brother," I said. "You know—*Aaaah!*"

She didn't react to that, either. Carrying on this one-sided conversation was beginning to bug me. What was I doing there anyway? It was bad enough to have gotten involved with him at the start, and hit him when I should have known better. Then I had to butt in when the kids were teasing him over his hat, and afterward pay the price of trying to be a hero. It all flooded over, making me warm, suggesting I ought to start minding my own business. But instead I got mad and when I get mad I get stubborn.

"Can't you talk?" I said annoyed. "There's no law against it."

Surprisingly, she nodded but I was still on the moon as far as she was concerned.

"Swell," I said quickly. "Where is he? The Dummy . . ."

The word slipped out. I was embarrassed, and thinking I'd ruined everything. But she lifted one hand and pointed into the distance over my shoulder. I waited a second in case she meant to break her vow and speak.

Nothing.

"Thanks a lot," I said, and turned away. Getting her to even wave was some kind of a breakthrough. Maybe someday she'd decide to say a word, and then eventually I'd find out the mystery of that crazy household.

I walked away from the house in the direction she had indicated, not that it meant much. I wasn't led to anything in particular, just some other buildings on the next street. He wasn't there. Her gesture hadn't been clear enough to tell me was he near or far away. I kept walking, wondering again if I wasn't the real Dummy after all.

I couldn't see him anywhere. I finally decided I would have to put myself in his shoes to find him, which meant stop and look at everything, and be led to other things. That was the way he moved along the street. I felt like some kind of two-legged bloodhound on the trail.

I found an old tennis sneaker and a concrete block.

67

Behind that was a fence with one board missing. I looked through the opening and saw a black and white cat licking its paw. The cat stopped to look at me and continued licking. It had that one paw awfully red but I suppose it knew what it was doing. Some dried tar was dribbled on the sidewalk. That led me to an oil slick in the street reflecting all the colors of the rainbow. I passed a street light with a chipped base. After that it was an old shoe with a busted shoelace speckled with white, blue and green paint. I noticed a doll without its head and one arm, a broken windshield wiper, a lady's purse with nothing in it. One manufacturing building had five broken windows. There were a lot of parked cars, one with a flat tire.

I had gone about five blocks and it looked like it might take forever to find the Dummy. Then I heard somebody yelling. I turned the corner and there he was.

He was standing in front of a bakery store looking very pale and frightened. A man, bald and fat, with a very red face and wearing a soiled-white long apron, had him by the arm and was practically screaming into the Dummy's ear. I thought I knew what had happened.

"Excuse me, mister," I said, interrupting.

He stopped yelling and looked at me angrily.

"What do you want?"

I pointed to the Dummy. "I think I know what the trouble is . . . "

He half-turned, shifting his feet, and shook his head impatiently.

68

"I got no time . . ." he barked. Then, "Who's asking for your two cents, kid? I got enough right here to . . ."

"You don't understand," I said quickly. "His mother works in a bakery a few blocks from here. She makes bread and stuff."

His thick eyebrows shot up. "She does? So what?"

I pointed to the Dummy who was watching me, mouth open. "He's kind of—well, he's not actually normal, you see. When he goes into her bakery, he takes all the cakes he can get his hands on. Nobody says anything. I guess he thinks all bakeries are the same."

The man's jaw dropped. He cocked his head and squinted down at me.

"Oh, yeah?"

"Is that what he was doing—taking your cakes without paying for them?"

The man rolled his eyes and grimaced. He let go of the Dummy's arm and mopped his forehead with a rumpled polka-dot blue handkerchief.

"Was he! He had half a dozen stuffed in his mouth and more in his pocket before I realized what was going on."

There might be a chance the Dummy understood what was going on.

"Is that what happened?" I asked him. I made the motions he had used—reaching for cakes, chewing some, putting some into my pocket.

His face lit up with that goofy smile.

"Aaaah," he said. He pointed to the store window

69

featuring a lot of cakes and the bakery sign. "My . . . my . . . " He put his hand in his pocket and drew out a soggy cake which he offered to me, bobbing his head. "You . . . you . . . eat . . . "

He pantomined his offer, chomping his jaws. The man was looking at both of us like he'd just discovered two morons instead of one, his lips twisted in a kind of disgust. I shook off the Dummy's offering.

"No, thanks." I turned to the bakery man. "You see? He can't help it. That's the way his mind works, mister."

The man grimaced and started to wave his fat arms. "For cryin' out loud! Why doesn't he stay the hell where he belongs then? Why don't they lock him up?"

I shrugged. "He's sick, I guess."

He waved his arms some more, almost dancing on the sidewalk.

"Go on—get him out of here. Get lost, both of you. Beat it!" I jerked my head to the Dummy. "Come on. Let's go home."

I turned and he was following. He looked at the store window as he passed, pointing at the display of cakes. "Aaah . . . aaah!"

"It's okay," I said. "Come on. I got something for you."

The man watched for a moment to make sure we were going, then blew out his cheeks, clapped himself on his bald head, and stomped back into his shop.

Around the corner I stopped and opened my paper bag. The Dummy's eyes widened and his lips parted when I drew out the little red drum. I put the strap around my neck and struck it a few times with the little white drumsticks.

"You like that?" I asked.

His head bobbed and he swallowed. "Aaaah," he said.

"Listen." I beat the drum again. "Rat-a-ta-tat," I said.

He looked at me blankly.

"I got it for you," I told him, taking the strap off my neck to put it over his, handing him the drumsticks. "Okay," I said. "Go on. Beat it. It's all yours."

He looked at me again without seeming to understand, so I took his hands holding the drumsticks and made them hit the drum.

"There you go," I said.

He still couldn't believe it. I had to smile, point to the drum, then to him, and say, "It's all yours. Your drum. I'm giving it to you. Go on. Play it. Play rat-a-ta-tat."

He looked at the drumsticks in his hands, then at the drum, then at me. It took him a while to digest the whole idea. He struck it gingerly with one of the sticks. He smiled at the sound and struck the drum with the other stick.

"Aaah," he said, smiling. "My . . . my . . ."

"It's a drum," I told him. "Maybe you'll call it rat-a-ta-tat."

He started banging away suddenly with both hands. No idea of rhythm, just banging away making noise. His eyes looked at me.

"That's the idea," I said. "Come on. Let's go home."

He banged the drum all the way there. First one hand, then the other, and then both together. By the time we got to his house my ears were tired. The porch was empty. The girl gone. I waved to the Dummy.

"Okay? Well, so long for now. I got to go."

He swung hard with both hands at the drum. "Boom boom," he said smiling.

"Right on," I told him. "Boom boom." I waved again and turned. "So long." Why couldn't I say his name? I knew it. I guess Alan Harper sounded too normal for him.

As I walked away I kept hearing the drum. When the sound didn't grow fainter I turned around. He was marching after me. I waved my hands and stopped. He stopped, too, his arms up ready to strike again.

"Look," I said. "Don't follow me. I'm going home."

He smiled and hit the drum. "Boom boom," he cried happily.

I shook my head and started off again. The drum beats came right on my heels. I stopped once more. So did he. I shook my head. He shook his. It was like we were playing Simon says.

"No," I said. "I got to go home. You stay. Come to think of it, maybe you ought to go home, too."

He smiled. Boom boom.

"No," I said. "Stay!"

As soon as I said it I realized it was like talking to a dog. What was the difference? He was following me home like one. I started walking faster, looking occasionally over my shoulder. He had increased his pace also. At the corner I ducked around and waited. Not for long.

Boom boom boom boom. And there he was again, smiling and patting the drum. "My . . . my," he said.

I had a quick feeling of panic sweep over me. I swear I felt like running. What good would that do? I tried once more, pointing back to where he lived.

"You go—home," I said. He looked at me smiling. I tapped my chest and pointed to the direction I was heading. "I go home, too. My home."

I felt like an Indian in a rotten TV movie.

He smiled, not understanding a word I had said, and hit the drum again and again.

"Boom boom," he said, his face lit up in that wide goofy smile.

There was nothing to do but keep walking and I managed that, my head hanging down.

"That's some friend you're picking up," I told myself. "You can't even invite him into your house."

I wondered briefly why I couldn't. One very good reason came back immediately: He wouldn't be welcome. And to tell the truth, I wasn't too sure I myself wanted him in our house. It wasn't that he was an alien, or black, or Chinese. His condition was worse than any of those. He was a moron. Doing a moron a little favor like giving him a drum wasn't such a big deal. The big question was could I live with one, and I knew the answer to that. A big no.

I got to my house, waved, and went inside feeling

ashamed. When I reached my room I looked out the window. I could see him standing there on the street. I could hear him, too.

Boom boom boom boom.

"Now you really did it, you dope," I told myself, and felt sick.

Boom boom.   My my red hit-nice-boom-boom.
My number one hit-boy

Walk   see things   hit hit my red boom boom
Walk . . . . . .   Soldier.
Round box boom.   Sticks   little sticks
Nice.   Nice hit.
Tell fly bird my nice red boom   Listen. Sing.
Song.   peep-peep-peep-peep   Nice.
Fly bird fly away   pretty fly bird   no go away.

Walk . . . . . . See things. Hit. Boom boom boom
                    boomboomboomboom.
Aaah.
My . . .   my place.   She.   My . . . Look look.
Boom boom.   More hit red boom boom . . .
                    my . . . my . . . she . . .
Sit down.   boom boom
She wet eyes. Up. Go away. No go. She run.
My . . . she away. Crying? Oh must be bad my red
boom boom hit stick.
Boom boom my my hit.   More hit hit.

10

I brought up the subject during dinner.

"How was that again?" my old man said, cupping his hand to his ear.

"I said how would it be if I brought a kid home? You know, like to visit? The trouble is, he's kind of dumb—sort of a moron."

"Sort of a what?" my old man asked.

"Moron. He's brain-damaged or something."

He whistled, unpleasantly. "Seems to me we got enough of that already around here without him."

"Thanks a lot. But can I?"

"Brain-damaged, did you say?" my mom said. She threw herself into a grotesque pose, arms and hands at awkward angles, making her face look stupid and drooly. "One of those kind?"

76

"Well, no. He's not like that. He looks normal but he's not. He can just say a word or two and doesn't understand much of what you say to him."

"Oh?" she said. "Well, then, what's the point, dear? I mean, if he can't talk and doesn't understand what you say—what's the point?"

I shrugged, feeling warm. "I don't know. I just wondered. He seems so—well, helpless."

She nodded. "Well, of course he would be. But why bring him here? You couldn't control him, could you?"

"Control?"

Her hands made aimless gestures. "Well, you know. Supposing he was doing something you wanted him not to. You said he didn't understand."

I had a quick mental image of the Dummy shoveling down those gooey cakes in the bakery. What if he got into our kitchen and found something he liked, could I stop him? Could anybody? I shook my head.

"Yeah. I guess you're right."

My old man got up and looked down at me, his lips twisting.

"Just so there won't be any mistake about it," he said between his teeth, "forget it. You want to be a hero, go to *his* house. I don't want any creepy characters like that in here. You get me?"

"He's not creepy . . . " I started to say.

"Forget it," he yelled, his face suddenly red and ugly, the big vein pulsing in his forehead. "They got places for misfits like that, and this house isn't one of them. Understand?"

I nodded, angry but feeling a quick mixed sense of relief and shame. The truth was, I didn't want him there myself.

"Yeah. Sure," I said.

Not satisfied, he leaned down close to me, his blue eyes hard, his mouth threatening. "Make sure you remember, smart guy. You got a young sister, don't forget."

I looked at him surprised. "So what?"

He jerked back as if I'd splashed water in his face.

"So what?" he repeated. "So what?" He passed his hand over his face, blew his cheeks out and groaned, rolling his eyes as though giving up on me completely. "So what?" he said again. Then shaking his head, thumping his leg with his rolled-up newspaper, he stomped out of the room. I could still hear him angrily talking to himself in the living room. "So what, he says!"

I looked across the table at Susie, wondering if she knew something I didn't. She shook her head blankly and turned to my mom. She jerked her head toward pop in the other room.

"What's with him?" Susie asked. "I know this Alan Harper, too. He's retarded. So what? He can't help it?"

Now suddenly my mom was screaming, her face red and angry too. "I don't want to hear any more about it. Don't you know anything?" She waited a moment, breathing hard. "Well, I can see that you don't, so I'm telling you now, once and for all time.

Your father is absolutely right. We don't want any creepy morons in this house. Don't you understand? They're dangerous!"

Susie started to laugh. "Dangerous? Him?"

It was a mistake. Mom brought her hand across the table in a stinging slap to Susie's cheek. "You heard me! And don't you ever laugh at me again when I'm telling you something for your own good and protection!"

Susie burst into tears, her face mottled red where she had been hit. She pushed her chair away and ran out of the room. I looked up at my mom mystified.

"Why did you do that?" I said.

She jammed her hands on her hips, stony-faced. Then she leaned forward and levelled a shaking finger at me.

"By rights, I should have given that one to you mister. It was your original bright idea. You're the smart alec who brought it up. Now you just pick yourself up and get out of here before I do something I might be sorry for."

Her face was ugly with anger, her lips twisted, her eyes wild. I didn't know what was bugging her, but I could see its effect. I pushed myself away from the table and walked out of the kitchen, still hearing her talking to herself.

"These damn kids don't know anything! Not a blessed damn thing! Would you believe it? Bringing me home a moron?"

Crazy, I thought. They were acting like they were

afraid of him. Suddenly I wondered how would they treat me if I was the Dummy? I saw myself moving like him, talking like him. I didn't have to think very long or hard about being him before I knew they'd be ashamed and angry. But would they also act frightened? I couldn't figure that part of it out yet. Still, there wasn't any doubt about my best chance around my own house: be and act normal. Otherwise? I didn't want to think about that.

I could hear Susie crying behind her closed bedroom door. I wanted to knock and tell her I was sorry I brought it up and she got hit. But I didn't. Everything had suddenly taken such a big turn, become so hysterical, I was afraid to discuss it.

I started to get a little angry with myself for ever getting wrapped up with him. *It's simple, you dope,* I told myself. *Make believe it never happened. Forget you ever met him. It's not your problem, is it?*

I was seeing again his bland face, the way he would blink suddenly and put on that goofy smile as if he just woke up. Then I imagined I heard him.

"Aaaah," he said. It made me mad.

Why did he have to be that helpless? Couldn't he do anything about it? Look at that dumb house he lived in, and that crazy sister and that nutty hardworking mother. They were all like rats in a trap, and what was worse they were beginning to nibble at me.

"Aaah," he said again.

This time I really blew my stack. "For cryin' out loud," I heard myself say under my breath, "say something else!"

I stormed outside. I had to find somebody to talk to, somebody who might get it straight in my head why anybody would hate somebody who was helpless, somebody you had to be sorry for. If my own folks felt that way what could I expect from anybody else?

I got on my bike hoping Mr. Alvarado would be home.

                        Up wet   *Up-*
What . . ?   Down   Nice.   Up-   oh very wet
         wet fall   *Down-*
wet-wet. All fall wet. On face wet. What nice wet?
                                   up   up
Walk in wet wet.   Tin-tin-tin-tin-tin
                             down   down
Oh what falling wet wet?
Shoe   put shoe in wet wet.   Oh no shoe
                             down down in wet.
Funny wet shoe make like . . . like . . . what wet
                                        down?
More shoe in wet wet.   All gone.
                         No shoe only wet wet.
Oh where shoe?
Hit wet wet   oh funny   face wet from wet wet
in eyes wet wet.
              up
        up
Look   there.   Sky.   Where sky?
No more sky.   Oh bad. All wet wet in sky.
No more my sky . . . my pretty blue . . . what?

Walk wet   walk-wet-wet   more walk more wet wet
Run-run-in-wet-wet   Oh how very   Too many
                                 wet wet.
                        up
Oh how very many wet wet . . . over me . . . my . . .
                                        all
                  down
everybody wet wet . . . All my things wet with
                                 wet wet.
Oh this very many wet wet fall.

11

It was still light when I pulled away from our house. Then it began to rain and the sky darkened. I didn't care.

"Go ahead. Rain," I told the soggy rain-clouds moving in. I guess so much thinking about the Dummy was catching; I was beginning to feel slightly nutty myself.

Mr. Alvarado lived in the Mexican-American barrio where most of the poor Chicanos lived and a few poor whites. It's a Spanish-speaking neighborhood made up mostly of small houses with little patches of lawn, some small apartments and a few tenements. Mr. Alvarado lived in one of the smaller apartment houses, a two-storey building, where I'd visited once after a game when he asked a few of us in for some lemonade, cake and ice cream. I always wanted to ask him why he lived there when he didn't have to.

It was dark when I arrived and I was soaked. I didn't see any kids playing on the wide street but I locked up my bike anyway. I needed wheels to get home. Mr. Alvarado's wife opened the door and asked me inside without batting an eye. The apartment was warm, bright and cheery. I looked down at the clean rug then at my wet sneakers, and began to wonder what I was doing there anyway, slopping up their place.

"It's all right," Mrs. Alvarado said quickly. "Rain is rain. You don't hurt anything. Come in, please. The baby's sick and I shouldn't keep the door open."

I noticed then she was holding her baby wrapped in a blue blanket, and though I couldn't see its face I heard it coughing.

"I'm sorry," I said, "I didn't mean to bust in like this but . . ."

"It's all right. You're one of Richard's boys, aren't you? He's in the kitchen. I'll get him."

She walked into the apartment while I was still fumbling for words to explain. I'd forgotten how pretty Mrs. Alvarado was; slender with dark hair, dark flashing eyes and a quick smile. She spoke quickly, too, and moved the same way. Women always look great in those black stockings.

I heard water running in the kitchen, then shut off, then their voices. I glanced around the living room. It looked more like a library, with books stacked everywhere, the walls crowded with paintings, and places on the bookshelves for little statues that looked hundreds of years old, Mexican gods and like that. There was a white sofa, some nice stuffed chairs, a lot of big lamps, a hi-fi set, low cocktail table, a TV console and a spinet piano. It didn't look much like a place in the ghetto area.

Mr. Alvarado came out of the kitchen drying a glass with a striped towel. He didn't look as big as he looked in class.

"Anything wrong, Neil?" he asked, glancing at me sharply.

I felt embarrassed suddenly. "Not too much. I'm sorry—I didn't know your baby was sick." I looked at the door. "Maybe some other time . . ."

Mrs. Alvarado came up behind him patting the baby's back.

"It's all right," she said. "I'm putting him to bed now." She peered at me. "He's wet, Richard. Give him that towel to dry off."

"Oh. Of course," Mr. Alvarado said, handing me the towel. "You are soaked, aren't you?" As I mopped some of the water off my face, he added: "You know Betty, don't you?"

"We met—that time you had a party," I said. "The ice cream, cake, lemonade, and like that."

"Oh, yes." He turned to her. "It's Neil Comstock, Betty. I won't be too long. There's nothing more we can do for the kid. We'll just have to sweat it out."

She nodded to me, smiled, and turned into a bedroom. I could hear the rasping cough of the baby as she closed the door.

"What's wrong with it?" I asked.

He shrugged. "A cold. I don't think it's too serious." I handed him back the towel and he motioned me to one of the stuffed chairs. "Whatever brought you all the way down here in the rain must be important. Sit down and tell me about it."

I felt chilled. "It's about the kid—the one I call the Dummy. The one I wrote about—when you thought I didn't do such a hot job telling about a character."

He drew a pipe from a rack, filled it and got it going. As he circled the match flame over the pipe bowl, he glanced at me.

"You didn't bike all the way down here to discuss a homework assignment."

"No, it's more complicated. I—I got to know him better. His name is Alan Harper. He looks about my age but ... "

Mr. Alvarado nodded. "Chronologically, he's thirteen and a half."

"Okay," I said. "A little older ... "

"He's mentally retarded, Neil. I checked his file after your essay. He has the mental development of a child of five. He's what is called an exceptional child. Brain damage."

"Exceptional?"

"That's the term used," he said. "We have no special

classes for MR or exceptional children at our school so we're trying to fit him into a program with younger children."

"You mean he's gonna stay that way—five?" *You got good reason to hate yourself*, I thought. *No wonder you felt rotten.* "He won't get any older—better?"

"Not very likely," Mr. Alvarado said. "Barring the possibility of a breakthrough with some new drug, he'll remain pretty much as he is now, and will always need care."

"Will he—do they—how about getting married, and so forth?" I asked.

"No way," Mr. Alvarado said. "Not a normal relationship anyway. Some of them, most really, require personal attention—nursing, medical, whatever—all their lives. He could, when mature, live with a nurse," Mr. Alvarado concluded. "It would depend on his growth, you see, and what the doctors conclude would be best for him. Or possible. They want these children to approximate some kind of normal living."

"Yeah," I said. "Oh, boy. That's a laugh."

He stared at me, pulling at his pipe. "As you say."

"How would it be if I brought him here—the Dummy?"

He shrugged. "Okay, I guess."

I glanced toward the closed bedroom door. "Even with the baby around?"

"Why not? Is he carrying a communicable disease?"

I remembered the scene at my house.

"I heard—aren't they supposed to be dangerous? I

88

mean, he doesn't hear too good, or maybe he doesn't understand. Anyway, aren't they hard to control?" He waited and I had to let it all out. "My folks told me tonight he was dangerous."

Mr. Alvarado smiled. "Helpless would be more like it. The only thing dangerous about children like Alan is their predicament. They have to be protected from hostile groups or individuals."

"That's what I thought," I said. "Only I figured, what did I know about anything? I got a feeling they're gonna kill him some day. He's so helpless . . . "

He leaned back and waved his pipe at me.

"I'd like to hear."

I told him all I knew about the whole set-up, the kids at school, the old man in the nut house, the sister who didn't talk, and the sly-eyed suspicious mother who didn't like to talk much either.

Mr. Alvarado nodded. "The father is being cared for at the State Psychological Institute. The mother works long hours and is the sole support of the family. The girl is classified as mentally retarded because she is autistic. She is able to talk but refuses to. Without her strange malady, Desdemona might be considered a gifted child, as many of them are. Perhaps some day, she'll respond to treatment."

"What's she got to talk about? If you ever saw where they lived, you'd know better. She's stuck with him—the Dummy—and her nutty old lady. I guess she feels the whole family is nuts. She's lucky her old man isn't around. If I was her, I don't know if I'd feel like talking either. That brother of hers is such a dumbbell —okay, I heard what you said, he can't help it—but just the same, if you gotta watch it all the time and live with it . . . "

Mr. Alvarado spread his hands apart.

"Don't get the idea that exceptional children are completely helpless. They can be trained for jobs, can carry out orders and execute them properly if so instructed. Some have strange but specific talents. I read of one recently who couldn't handle the buttons on his clothes or tie his shoes, but was gifted musically. He was able to coordinate his brain and fingers playing the piano and had almost fifty musical pieces he remembered and could play. That's pretty good for a kid who can't tie a knot in his shoes."

"They got no piano where he lives," I said. "All they got is some old junky furniture, a lot of sloppy clothes all over the place, and drawers full of the cakes he grabs from the bakery where his mother works."

Mr. Alvarado leaned back and looked at me.

"What's your point—poverty? Have you walked around this neighborhood? This is the barrio, you know. The ghetto. Here is where you find the underprivileged, the undernourished, the uneducated, the unemployed, the unwanted." His dark eyes glowed. "Not brain-damaged. Normal human beings. Decent people. There's a lot of misery here, too, and you don't have to look too hard to find it."

"But they weren't born crippled . . . "

He smiled. "Crippled in what way, Neil? In the

head? That's not the only place where it hurts. Here it's race, skin. Born brown. Across the barrio born black. Bodies normal, brains unscrambled. No short circuits, barring a few exceptions, accidents of birth, what have you. But they can't function as normal human beings. They can't develop, flower—don't you see? Once you cannot function within your potential you're crippled, too."

I looked around the apartment, then back at him.

"You're Mexican," I said. "You got educated. You made it."

He slumped back in his chair.

"Yes. I made it. And Betty made it. The baby—he's got a good chance, too." He got to his feet. "Excuse me a moment, I want to see how he's doing. He's got a bad cough."

He came back in a few minutes.

"He's asleep now. Betty has to stay with him a little while longer. I'm sorry because I'd like her to be in on this conversation, too. Perhaps she might help with your problem."

"It's okay," I said. "At first I thought it was his problem, not mine."

"Not any more, Neil. You've begun to feel a certain responsibility for it. I'm still trying to understand that. You seem to be tying up his mental condition with his family and the neglect of his home. You have to understand it could happen to any child anywhere. It could have happened to me, to you— anybody. The same goes for his sister. It may be a chemical imbalance in the brain, something that went haywire somehow. Nobody knows why, for certain. They're still working on it. They used to blame the parents. Now they're not so sure. Some children have come out of it. A lot more haven't. There's always hope and that's what we live with."

"I don't even know if he can read," I said. "He can hardly talk. He seems to want to but he can't think of the words."

Mr. Alvarado shrugged. "Sometimes these children are good at certain games. They like singing, dancing, sports."

I had a picture of the way he ran, how he couldn't seem to get out of the way of his own two feet.

"He can whistle pretty good. But that's about all."

Mr. Alvarado smiled gently and lifted his hands.

"Well, then, being able to whistle is something, isn't it?"

"I suppose. He walks okay. He looks at a lot things. That's how he spends his time. But it's like he doesn't know he's got two hands or that they belong to him, except when he's eating and finds something in them."

"That's typical, too," he said. "Part of the same short circuit in the brain. Some of these children are especially vulnerable from the rear. They have no awareness of anything behind them."

I remembered how helpless he had been when the kids grabbed his hat and pushed him around and tripped him.

"That's for sure. But I don't see how he's going to cut it in school."

Mr. Alvarado frowned. "In the state of California, brain-damaged children are regarded as neurologically handicapped. School is not mandatory for them as it is for the blind, deaf, crippled or mentally retarded. It's permissive—school districts can provide education if they so choose. At our school they're trying to fit Alan in with normal children of a lower age. Sometimes they adjust and the experience is good for all. But there are special private schools for children with his handicap. Do you understand?"

"Sure," I said. "You're telling me if you're brain-damaged, you better be sure you're rich, too."

Mr. Alvarado shrugged. "It's up to the citizens who live here. They turned down the new school bond issue to make the schools safe against earthquake damage. It would have cost them thirty-two cents a year extra to insure the safety of their own kids—not enough of them voted for it. Maybe after the next quake, after they dig out a few children from the rubble, they may decide it's worth the extra thirty-two cents."

Mr. Alvarado seemed to know a lot about the whole subject, and probably had been through it all before so didn't get excited anymore. I went over what happened at my house earlier.

"It bugged me because I didn't know what I was talking about. Like facts. I wasn't sure how I felt then. When they flew off the handle and said I couldn't bring him in the house because he was dangerous, I first got mad. Afterward, I felt sort of relieved—when they said there was no way. I thought I wanted him

93

over—and then saw I really didn't. It was like a cop-out, blaming them. I didn't want him anyway."

"That's only natural, Neil. You're trying to take hold of a situation that you neither understand nor are equipped to handle. Brain-damage cases—the mentally retarded—they're spooky. When we're ignorant, we're afraid. And when we're afraid, we're lost."

I looked down at my wet sneakers. They had stained the carpet underneath, but Mr. Alvarado didn't appear to notice.

"That's what I wanted to know," I said, feeling my throat tighten. "Why? The fact that I really wasn't too keen about having him, either, yet making this big stink like I really wanted him. Like he really was my friend."

He nodded. "Normal, too. It's a typical reaction to an unfamiliar subject. You've nothing to be ashamed of. You're bright and normal, sensitive, fast-thinking, athletic and fast-moving. Everything Alan Harper isn't."

"He's such a lump," I said. "Such a meatball. I didn't even know he was a real Dummy when I first laid the name on him."

Mr. Alvarado nodded, then got up and stretched. He tapped his pipe out into an ashtray.

"You've made a lot of progress since your report. I can appreciate your sympathy but I don't recommend your taking Alan's problem. Frankly, it's too much for you. Perhaps it might be better for you and your family if you sort of eased off, disengaged . . . "

"You mean, forget about him?"

94

He shrugged. "I doubt you can do that, not just yet. It's still a raw, new, and totally different experience for you. But I'm very pleased with this forward step you've taken."

"Oh, yeah? Which one is that?"

"Involvement," Mr. Alvarado said.

Hello how are you?   *Hello how are you?*
My hit-boom boom . . .   *Oh boom*   *hit hit*

Boy. One more boy. Kick-throw-run-funny-
                                what boys.
Oh   my   *Bad very bad . . .*
Take my red boom-hit.   *Run-run*
Oh too-much-run-run . . .   *No more boom boom*
My red hit-hit-number-one-boy-boom hit.
My . . .   Look   look   Oh where
Aaah   My . . . Number one hit-boy. Aah.
My my red what.   Oh . . . . . . why run?

Many things.
Hit my boom boom red what.

12

I decided I would take Mr. Alvarado's advice
and try easing off with the Dummy. What he called
disengage. It wasn't hard. I had a lot of homework,
so that helped take my mind off. The next few days,
whenever I did happen to think of him, I told myself
right away, "So what?" and quickly thought about
something else. Like what a nice day it was, how the
Dodgers were doing, or how I was going to get some
money together to see the first game of the Rams. I
didn't once bring up the subject at home, and Susie
laid off and didn't give me a hard time about her getting smacked because of my bright ideas. I didn't even
catch a cold after getting all soaked on that crazy ride
over to see Mr. Alvarado. I caught heck, of course,
for going out but it didn't kill me.

We were let out of school early one day. Some big deal end-of-the-term teacher conference fouled things up, so we got a break. I brought my school books home and then went down to the corner lot figuring I'd run into some of the guys like Dave and Charley and we'd have some fun. I heard them yelling and whooping it up before I turned the corner. I broke into a run figuring I'd surprise them and grab the ball. Then I saw what all the fun was about and slowed down.

There were three kids on the field—Dave, Charley and, in between, the Dummy. Dave tossed something over the Dummy's head to Charley, something that turned slowly in the air, spinning red and white. There was a *thunk* as it struck Charley's hands, and even though I was still some distance away I heard the Dummy's bleating cry. They went down the field, tossing the drum back and forth over his head, side to side in front of him and behind him, and he stumbled along, arms outstretched, trying to keep up, to stop and pivot when they did, trying to guess which way they'd throw it, tripping all over himself. It was the same old game of tease, different this time because my own friends were in it. By the way I suddenly felt so rotten, all over again, I knew how good had been the last few days of disengagement, according to Mr. Alvarado.

Dave saw me first. He waited until I got close, then side-stepped quickly behind the Dummy. Charley, after first feinting the Dummy out of position, making believe he was going to toss it low, lobbed the drum over his head. Dave caught it and held it out, tantalizing. The Dummy reached and Dave threw it over his head to me.

The Dummy turned, reaching out automatically for his drum, saw me and froze, his mouth open, eyes wide with surprise. He looked at the little red drum in my hands as if he didn't quite understand, then back into my face.

"It's supposed to be a game," I told him. "It's a lot of fun. We throw it back and forth and you're supposed to keep after it till you get it."

He blinked, puzzled. Dave slipped behind him, signalled me with his hand and I tossed the drum over the Dummy's head. He never moved. He kept staring at me as if he couldn't believe I was for real.

"Aaaah," he said.

"It's not serious," I told him. "It's a lot of fun. It's a game. You want some fun in your life, don't you?"

He looked at me, not understanding.

"It's a game," I yelled. "Fun." I spelled it for him. "F-u-n, fun. Don't you want fun?"

He blinked. He looked down at his hands as if noticing for the first time they were empty.

"My . . . " he said. "My . . . "

Charley and Dave were flipping the drum back and forth. I raised my hand and Charley flipped it to me. I held it out to the Dummy. He smiled that big goofy smile.

"Aaah. My . . . my . . . "

As he reached for it, I whipped the drum behind my back. He looked down at his hands puzzled. I took it from behind me again and showed it to him.

"It's a game, don't you get it?" I said, mad.

He held his hands out and turned them over as if expecting the drum to show up on the other side.

"Aaah," he said. "No . . . no . . . no my . . . "

"I got it," I said. "Right here. Do you want it?"

He smiled again and reached for it. As his hands almost touched the drum, I let it fall to the ground between us. He looked at his hands again, then at me. I couldn't take it any more. I bent and scooped the drum up and jammed it into his chest.

"Here. You got it?"

His arms cradled the toy. He looked happy enough to cry, like I'd done him the world's biggest favor.

"My . . . my . . . " he said. Then he held it out for me to see.

"Okay," I said. "Okay. It's all yours. Forget about the game and all the fun."

Charley whistled and suddenly darted forward. As he was about to grab the drum out of the Dummy's hand, I wheeled and tripped him. He fell, looking up at me surprised.

"What's with you?" he asked.

I shook my head, my throat too tight to speak decently.

"Don't you get it? He's only a Dummy. He don't understand."

"So what?" Dave said.

He jumped forward and grabbed the drum out of the Dummy's hands. The Dummy made his favorite sound. I whirled, batted the drum away from Dave, and scooped it off the ground on the bounce. I held it against my chest now, mad at both of them, mad at the Dummy, even mad at myself.

"It's the Dummy's drum," I said. "I gave it to him. My pop gave it to me only I'm too old for it now."

"So what?" Dave said.

He broke into his jogging run, the hook pattern for a pass, signalling with his hand where he wanted it tossed. I wished Dave hadn't done that. I shook my head, turned my back to him, and handed the Dummy the drum.

"Here. Hold on to it, for cryin' out loud," I said.

"Aaah." He was smiling again.

Dave circled back, his face sweating. He stared at me and at the drum in the kid's hands. Charley got up and finished knocking the dirt off his pants. He looked at me, too, without a word.

"He trusts me," I said. "I guess I'm his only friend."

Dave and Charley exchanged glances like I'd suddenly flipped.

Dave let out a long low whistle.

"Okay, Dummy. You keep him," he told me.

"Yeah," Charley said. "So long, you Dummy-lover."

They started walking quickly away.

"Oh, come on," I said. "He don't dig the game. The drum is all he's got. Just a crummy little kid's drum."

I watched them go until they were at the far end

of the field. Something touched my arm and I jumped. It was the Dummy, holding his drum out to me.

"My," he said smiling. "My . . . my red . . . what," and held out his drumsticks to me.

I pushed his arm away. "Oh, get lost!" I said savagely, feeling sick inside.

My angry words bounced off him without effect. He smiled.

"Oh get lost. Oh get lost." Then he hit the drum. "Boom boom." Then he put it all together for me. "Boom boom. Oh get lost. Boom boom. Oh get lost."

He kept on beating the drum, repeating the words in cadence without understanding. I looked over his shoulder. Dave and Charley weren't waiting for me. They were my best friends and now I'd blown them. I felt like smacking the Dummy. A quick picture of Mr. Alvarado floated into my mind. He was looking anxious and worried over the baby coughing and still trying to pay some attention to me. "*I can appreciate your sympathy,*" he was saying, "*but I don't recommend your taking on Alan's problem. Frankly, it's too much for you.*"

I nodded, biting my lip. "You can say that again," I muttered.

"Boom boom. Oh get lost," the Dummy was yelling.

"*Perhaps it might be better for you and your family if you sort of eased off, disengaged . . .*

"Yeah, sure," I said. "How do you do that? You didn't tell me how to do that."

"But I'm very pleased with this forward step you've taken."

"Yeah," I said. "Me, too. I can't begin to tell you how happy it's made me."

"Involvement," Mr. Alvarado said, his eyes large, black and very intense. The words repeated themselves as if they had become stuck in an echo chamber. *"Involvement involvement involvement."*

There was a blur in front of my eyes. The Dummy was marching around me in a tight circle, banging the little drum every other step.

"Boom boom. Oh get lost. Boom boom. Oh get lost."

"I needed you like a hole in the head, you dummy," I told him.

He smiled happily and kept on marching, chanting, beating that stupid drum to death.

I could see Dave and Charley in the distance. Maybe I could still catch up to them and explain. I started off fast and suddenly stopped. What was there to explain?

The Dummy came at me again marching like a stiff toy soldier. "Oh, get lost. Boom boom," he said.

Now, what? I asked myself. *What do you do now, stupid? Are you going to spend the rest of your life being a Dummy-lover? Even Mr. Alvarado told you about disengaging, right? So do it. Disengage. Are you your dummy-brother's keeper?*

Then I was running again, hoping Dave and Charley would be waiting for me around the corner, laughing when I caught up to them, and we'd all have a big special laugh about that dumb Dummy. I could hear him still behind me and I ran faster, running so hard I finally couldn't hear anything but the sound of my feet digging into the ground and my gasping breath. The wind felt soft and good on my face and I could tell right away that was the secret. That was all there was to it.

All I had to do was keep on running.

On a sunny day   On a sunny day
Will you pay attention.
                        Will-you   will-you   will-you
You are not trying, Alan.   Alan.
                            Pay attention, Alan.
Oh look on sunny day . . .
                    br . . rr . r birds out   flap-flap
Tree
You must pay attention.   Look here please.
                                    Clap-clap . . .
Oh pretty br . . rr . . r bird fly in sky . . .
                        way up to white thing . . .
If-you-do-not   if-you-do-not
                    oh pay attention   then-I-
will-have-to-put . . .
Eyes.   I see eyes   Everybody.
                        Lady eyes.   In face eyes.
Up
            there.   One eye.   One more eye.
                    Blink blink. Oh how funny eyes.
What thing?   What other thing?
                        There thing under eyes.
Nose?   My . . . nose.   Feel nose.
                            Push nose.
Oh look inside nose there . . .
                    finger . . . pocket . . . nose . . .

Up up.   Get up please.
                    Will you stand up please.
Now-will-you   now-will-you . . .

Oh look there on glass   white what?

                                   Butter-thing.

Fly away butter-white-thing
up-   up-
    down   down . . .
No more butter-white-thing . . .
Now I have had enough   do-you-hear
do-you   stand-up-please . . .
A very nice   sunny   day.
Say goodbye boys-and-girls please.

13

I guess that was the week I started cracking up. No matter how many times I told myself the Dummy wasn't my affair, and I could be a lot happier not knowing about him, it didn't work. He kept sneaking back into my thoughts when I would least expect him. I'd no sooner finish telling myself, "Okay, forget you ever laid eyes on him. Okay? He's not there. You never heard of him," and there he'd be, right in front of my eyes, inside my head, giving me that dumb look and that goofy "Aaaah". I'd see him that way all day and at night, coming right between thoughts that were a million miles away from him. Like, thinking of a book I ought to read, and there he'd be. Like looking in a store window, not a bakery, and hearing his voice, seeing his face. I suppose I just didn't have enough willpower. Anyway, no matter how I tried to disengage myself, as Mr. Alvarado had suggested, it didn't work. The Dummy hung on like a bad dream.

Outside it was different. I didn't see him anywhere and I didn't go looking for him. I even stayed away from his old lady's bakery just to play it safe, and gave up on jelly doughnuts.

I wanted to ask Mr. Alvarado about this at school. But Mr. Alvarado apparently was a lot better at this disengaging business than I was. He looked right through me. He didn't ask me how I was doing about disengaging, either. It appeared to have slipped his mind, and me along with it. He looked tired and more gloomy than usual, and I figured the sick baby was keeping him up a lot nights and robbing him of his sleep.

On the way home from school I found myself looking at different things the way the Dummy did, staring at poles and street lamps as if I expected them to start dancing or something. I'd shuffle along vacant lots peering down at a lot of junk, toeing them over with my shoe and examining them like I was looking for diamonds. I found a lot of grub worms that way and about a million rotting things, but it was worth it when I came across something interesting and pretty. It could be something as simple as a broken beer bottle, for Pete's sake. Hunkered over it, I saw captured rainbow colors and strange shapes that didn't look like anything I had ever seen before or even knew about. They were like pieces of dreams that didn't fit together, not making any sense, but disturbing, making me wonder who I was and what I was doing there anyway. I'm really surprised I wasn't picked up as some kind of derelict ragpicker and sent away to get myself cured. When I got home I had to take a shower, soap myself three times over, and change my clothes before they'd let me eat with them.

Susie didn't say anything but kept looking like she expected to find I'd brought a dead cat home. I heard my mom complaining to my pop about it, how I was coming home stinking and dirty, and what were they going to do about it, for God's sake? He listened for a while, while she said most of it over twice, then I heard his familiar mocking growl.

"It's okay," he said. "Maybe he'll be a garbageman someday. I guess we can always use a good garbageman in this town. He's always had the mentality for it anyway." But he didn't say a word to me directly. I suppose he couldn't stand the smell or the sight of me.

I didn't see much of Charley or Dave after the drum incident. If they thought I was nuts that time for sticking up for the Dummy they'd think I was a lot nuttier if they saw me wandering around looking and staring, even talking at things. I suppose those times were my closest to the Dummy. I knew he couldn't tell what half the things he saw really were and, even if he knew, wasn't able to name them right.

I'd be looking at a knothole in a fence, looking at it like I was seeing it for the first time in my life. "Knothole," I'd say. Then before I knew it, I was trying out other things the Dummy might be saying. "Ho . . . ho . . ." or maybe "My nice ho." Instead of fence I said, "Fen," and in case that was too much said, "Woo woo," like he described wood. It got to be no problem after a while and I could half-describe almost anything I saw. I even could do it to myself. I'd start the walk at age twelve and finish talking like a six-year-old.

I don't know exactly why I did it. I suppose to get the feeling of how it was to go through life like the Dummy. But it was all fake, all an act, because I could snap out of it any time I liked and be myself.

I didn't let anybody grab my hat or push me around. I was too chicken for that. I didn't stuff myself with cake and junk the way he did, either, but I did manage to make myself kind of slow-witted and dumb when I wandered around. I even said "Aaah" a couple of times to get the right feeling of being him.

So I had this thing going for a while, stumbling and bumbling around all by myself while pretending to be the Dummy. Nobody ever caught on, or saw me; nobody I knew anyway. Until one day, really caught up in it, I forgot to be careful and look around once in a while. I had just finished examining a piece of wire like I intended setting the crown jewels in it when I looked up and there she was.

Desdemona. The Dummy's silent sister.

She was standing near a fence at the other end of the lot when our eyes met. We both jerked back and stiffened like we'd been caught by the same lightning bolt. Before I had a chance to say anything she'd slipped away behind the fence. Feeling like an awful jerk, I started to run after her, then stopped, realizing that whatever I'd say would sound twice as dumb. She'd never understand. She wouldn't answer, either, I'd be worse off than ever in her eyes, and never know what she thought.

I went home feeling shook up.

How could I explain why I was imitating him and make sense of it? I wasn't sure even I understood why. But having her see me doing it made me feel ashamed, and I told myself angrily that was the end. I wasn't going to play Dummy any more. If he kept coming into my thoughts, well, I couldn't help that.

But that doesn't mean you got to be the Dummy, I told myself. *So forget it.*

I agreed that was good advice. Then in a flash I saw myself as him being held by the angry bald-headed red-faced man who owned the other bakery, having my arm shaken and twisted. It hurt. And all the cakes in my pocket were beginning to get squashed. I got very excited.

"Aaaah," I said.

That's when I first got scared. Because the word came out without my meaning it to, like I really was the Dummy this time, not merely pretending to be. My arm hurt like the man had actually twisted it. I had to rub the pain away. I almost stumbled over to my mirror. What I saw in it was me, all right, looking pretty much the same except my face was glistening with sweat.

"Are you for real?" I asked myself.

I went to bed trying to tell myself I just had a very vivid imagination, that that was all. I didn't really want any part of being a Dummy. My old man already thought I had the brains of a garbageman, and I was in enough trouble without asking for any more.

I had difficulty dropping off to sleep. In my dreams I was running and running with a lot of people chasing me.

"He's the one!" somebody yelled. "He's the one who did it!"

I never found out who yelled or what I was supposed to have done. I woke up scared, soaked with sweat, and pinched myself to make sure I was awake. I felt the pinches, so that meant it was me there, all right. After a while I dozed off and slept the rest of the night through without dreaming.

When I woke up it was still half dark outside. I tiptoed to the mirror to see what there was to see.

It was me, and no imitation.

Outside.   Walk walk . . .
Things.   See things.   Oh many things.
Girl . . .   little girl.   Play with ball.
Nice little girl.
More play   play . . .   Roll.   Roll ball.
Catch.   Catch ball . . .
Man   bad man.   Talk
talk mad.   No like . . .
Bad man take ball   little-girl-ball.   Cry.
Girl crying.   Bad man hit.
Oh how very bad hit little girl . . .
Now mad me . . .   hit . . .   Run.
Oh run-so-very-fast.
Why bad man hit little girl so?

People   many people   boys
girls . . . .
Say loud come back here you.
Run-run too-much-run Oh-hurt-my . . .   Run . . .
She.   She there house   My . . .
my she look . . . . . no-talk look . . .
Throw-things-people   hard hurt things
Oh, how very bad.   Hide.   No look.
No want hurt from things-people . . .
Oh   boy . . .
my number one hit-funny-what-give-hat-back-give-
red-boom-boom-stick-oh-get-lost-oh-get-lost boy.
Come here please   I won't hurt you.
You must   you must . . .

We ...   We.   Run around.   Out around.
Look at all those.
Why throw-hit she?   Oh how bad ...
Make smoke   all   around.   Hurt-eyes smoke.

Ride ...
Nice look out window ...... move-trees-things
ride.
a bus ... bus.
Go out.   Walk walk ...
Wait here please, I will see ...
I will talk to him ...
He-will   he-will   he-will-know-what ...
Oh yes wait.

Number-one say come   again   Let us go
Hurry please hurry ...
In here now.   Get in here
so-they-never-will ...
Oh dark in ...

14

It was mid-afternoon. I was home lying on the bed trying to make up my mind whether to be like Roman Gabriel of the L. A. Rams or Jerry West of the Lakers. I had read someplace that, to get anywhere in life, you had to set an early goal for yourself. I liked the idea of being a star quarterback like Gabe and throwing the long bombs for the winning touchdowns. It seemed a lot simpler than the way Jerry West worked. Jerry always came through in the clutch and made the basket, but then the other team would spark and get hot, and all those clutch plays would go out the window. When the team worked together it was fine, but you knew West couldn't keep saving the game every time he stole the ball. Gabe had to do his thing right just a few times and that was it. The more I thought, the more I was inclined to go for Gabe's position. All I had to do was grow about another foot, put on another hundred pounds, and have the coach give me a chance. I was wondering how to go about convincing him I could make the grade when Susie burst into the house.

She was crying and breathless when she reached my room.

"They're after him!" she cried. "You've got to do something."

Knowing Susie's big imagination, I didn't jump right into the air.

"After who?" I asked lazily.

"Your friend. Alan. The Dummy!"

I sat up.

"After him for what? Are you telling the truth for once?"

She nodded, gulping, trying to catch her breath.

"It's a whole mob of people—kids, grown-ups, every-body."

It didn't seem like one of her patent fairytales.

"Why? What's he supposed to have done?"

"Murdered a little girl in the park."

I was on my feet, my mouth open. "Murdered a little girl? He couldn't do that."

"I know," she said. "Well, maybe he didn't exactly murder her. I mean, I just saw her lying there, her clothes torn, and she looked awful bloody."

"Holy cow!" I yelled. "Why don't they call the police?"

She shrugged. "I guess no one thought of that yet. They were all out to get him. It seems somebody saw him running away just a little while before they found the little girl there."

I was sweating to get my sneakers back on.

"He wouldn't do that. Maybe he was running away because he got scared."

"I know," Susie said. "I tried to tell them that and they—hit me."

I was on my way out the door, yelling, "Maybe you can find a cop. I don't know if I can get there in time."

I knew a shortcut to his house and I ran harder than ever in my life. About a block away I could hear a swelling sound, and see them coming from the park and the side streets, some running and cheering, if you can imagine that. His sister was sitting on the porch, her face framed in her hands, looking out into space as usual.

"Where is he?" I yelled as I came up the walk.

She didn't bat an eye.

"Come on!" I cried. "He's in trouble and I got to help him." Her eyes shifted to mine. She could hear all right. I gestured down the street. "Don't you hear them? That's what I'm talking about. Wake up. will you—this is an emergency. They'll rip him apart."

She turned her head, her expression changing. Her hands fell to her sides and she stiffened.

"Go on," I yelled. "Stand up—get a better look—and then tell me where he is!"

She stood looking toward the corner, her face averted, staring at the oncoming rabble, and she swung one arm behind her, finger pointing toward the door.

"Thanks. You better get away yourself. You may not be safe, either."

Her dark eyes flashed and she gave me a look of contempt. I couldn't spare time arguing with her, so I shrugged it off and ran into the house. In the darkness there I bumped into a lot of furniture. It was like fighting my way through a jungle at night, and I got mad.

"Hey, you in there any place?"

I heard him before I saw him.

Boom. Boom.

Only a Dummy like him, I told myself, could play a drum at a time like this. His face lit up when he saw me and he gave me that goofy smile. I didn't have time to be polite and grabbed his arm.

"Come on. You're in big trouble."

He bobbed his head and smiled happily. He started to beat the drum again and I shifted my grip to hold his hands. He opened his mouth, looking hurt.

"Not now," I told him. "We got to get you out of here. Is there another door somewhere?" He stared at me, not understanding a word. "Door. Door," I yelled. "Side door? Back door?" He kept on staring and I pantomimed knocking on a door, turning the knob and opening it. "Door—door. Where is other door?" I asked excitedly.

He clapped his hands, his face lighting up. He

pointed left, toward the kitchen. "My . . . my . . . "

Did he know what he was talking about? The kitchen had a back door, all right. So I pulled him to his feet and pushed him along toward it.

"Let's go. Don't argue."

The back yard was small, piled high with all kinds of junk, weeds ten feet tall, and underneath a sagging clothesline on the ground all the sheets and things supposed to be hung up drying. I pushed him ahead of me through a loose board in the fence. He started to wander off and I grabbed him once more and pulled him close.

"Come on," I told him. "Be nice."

"Nice. Nice," he said, reaching out to pat my chest.

"Yeah. Sure. Come on. I gotta see what's happening out front with your daredevil sister."

I heard the mob yelling as we sneaked along the side. They were a lot closer now but the wild undergrowth of the Dummy's front yard kept us hidden. His sister was standing on the porch facing them, her head thrown back defiantly, her fists jammed into her hips.

Some jerk in the mob called out, "Where is he?" And the others all started shouting for her to bring him out.

She listened a while, looking them over silently, then slowly extended her arm directly toward them, thumb up. She wagged that thumb at them and then jerked it up twice, contemptuously.

They didn't like that. Suddenly there was a sharp crack of a stone bouncing off the door behind her. It brought a shout of approval from the other morons in the crowd. Soon the air was filled with rocks and stones, all bouncing around the Dummy's sister. Then her luck ran out. One rock caught her flush on the forehead. She swayed and staggered back but didn't fall. The crowd yelled. I couldn't believe it. If it had struck her down dead they would have been happy.

I felt like a Dummy myself standing there, trying to make up my mind what to do, besides sending her some telepathy.

"Run, run," I urged her silently. "You can't trust those jerks."

It didn't work. She continued to stand her ground under the hail of stones, getting hit, not even bothering to duck. Then I heard the wail of a prowl car and felt better. The stones stopped falling as the car came up and the crowd quieted. When two husky cops got out they didn't need to use a bullhorn, they just plowed a path through to the house. Desdemona was finally down, swaying back and forth on her haunches, staring out into space without any expression, blood streaming down her thin face.

Some jerky kid jumped out in front of the cops and yelled, "She's hiding him in there."

The first cop looked at him with no expression and rapped him in the mouth with his nightstick. It was the first time I ever enjoyed seeing a cop hit somebody.

I felt a tap on my shoulder. The Dummy was rocking back and forth, his mouth open, trying to form words he couldn't say.

"Oh, how bad," he said finally. "Oh, how very very." Then he pointed ahead. "Why make smoke?"

I'd smelled it, but being so scared and nervous hadn't noticed what was going on. Now I saw little licks of flame coming out of the bushes where some idiot had started to try burning their house down. From the distance I heard the sharp hooting of a fire engine heading our way.

When I turned back to tell the Dummy everything would be okay now, he was gone. I saw him across the street, ran and caught up with him, and tried to pull him back. But he was very strong and kept on running. Around the corner, out of sight of the crowd, I got ahead of him and threw up my hands to block him. He ran right into me and we crashed together into the wall of an auto-body shop. He liked that and smiled while I rubbed the back of my head.

"It's okay," I told him. "Your sister will be okay. Understand?" His eyes didn't tell me anything. "You're the one with the big problem," I said "What are we going to do about you? You're in trouble. Do you know that?"

He tapped his chest proudly. "Me. Me. I. My. Mine."

I was in way over my head and knew it but couldn't do anything about it. I didn't dare take him back to the police with that mob of nuts around. They'd kill both of us before we ever got there.

"About that little girl who got hurt in the park," I said, "did you do anything? Did you hurt her?"

He looked at me blankly, then smiled, seizing the one word he could dig. "You, you," he said happily. He pointed at me. "You. My . . . my . . . you."

I looked at him and felt my body slump. How was I going to help him? I couldn't hide him any place and depend on him staying there. I couldn't take him to my house; that would only start another riot. I stood there looking at the Dummy, rubbing my dumb head and hoping for a miracle idea. Then I remembered how friendly to the downtrodden Mr. Alvarado was. There was a bus stop a few blocks away and I still had my allowance money on me.

"Come on," I told the Dummy. "I think I know somebody who can help us."

He bobbed his head as if he understood. Then he snapped his drumsticks out suddenly and before I could stop him he was beating the little red drum.

"Boom boom," he said happily.

I could tell that long bus ride ahead of us was going to be some fun.

I am not   *I am not*

You stay now. Do you hear? Do you . . . . . you . . . ?
Don't forget   do you.
Up door.   Number-one.   My number-one-hit-
hurt-kick-funny-what-help-hat-red-boom-boom-. .
house-door-ride-wait-ride-big-car. . .
Walk . . .
Wait outside, you hear now?   Wait now.

Things. Walk to things . . . Oh how many. Nice . . .
Then   I am not.   Oh where . .?
Where number-one boy?

Hello how are you   how are you today?
Faces.   Yes-faces.   Play red boom sticks.
Number-one run-run-talk . . . where the hell you go
*   Dummy.*
Dint I say   Dint I?   Now look . . . . . . trouble.

15

"You did what?" Mr. Alvarado said.

I told him again. He didn't look any happier.

"You brought him here? Where is he?"

"Downstairs. I told him to wait until I had a chance to talk to you."

"But you had no right . . . " He opened the door and looked out "Downstairs, did you say?"

"Yes, sir. I didn't want to bring him in before you said it would be okay."

"But you can't . . . " Mr. Alvarado tugged at his hair. His lips twisted and he took a couple of deep breaths. "Don't you understand? The authorities will be looking for him."

"I guess so," I said. "But that's the whole idea. He didn't do anything, I swear. He couldn't. I mean, he's a Dummy and all that but he couldn't hurt anybody."

"You can't be sure," Mr. Alvarado snapped. "Nobody can be that sure. Least of all you. What experience have you had with this kind of problem?"

"None," I admitted, beginning to worry. "Except that I got to kind of know him lately, and how he thinks. He's really afraid of people. It's just things that he likes to get close to."

"Things?"

"Yes, sir."

Mr. Alvarado didn't seem to be responding the way I expected.

"Ridiculous," he said. "It would take a qualified psychiatrist to make a value judgment. I'm not saying the boy is criminally insane or that he might have done this terrible thing. I just don't know. And as for you foisting your opinion on me, you simply aren't capable of making that kind of judgment. He might have done it, just as he might not have. It's up to the proper authorities to say."

I heard coughing sounds behind the closed bedroom door, and figured that was partly the reason Mr. Alvarado was so nervous.

"I just figured if I kept him safe for a few days, or only a little while—until they found the guy who did it . . ." I offered.

Mr. Alvarado threw up his hands and started pacing the room.

"You want me to be an accessory to a crime? To take him in? Me? Here in the barrio? Do you know the trouble we've already had here with the police? The Mexican community is totally without representation. They can walk right in and slaughter us any time they wish. Don't you read the newspapers? Perhaps you watch TV then—it was all over their screens the past few weeks. The police simply walked right in and shot two innocent Mexicanos. Don't you know anything?"

I was too bewildered to speak. I suppose it is dumb not to follow politics more closely. I'd heard something about that shootout, but not enough to know really what it was all about. The sheriff's men, looking for some dope pushers, came to the wrong house and started shooting. Somebody had told them these men were armed and dangerous. Something like that. And two Mexicanos got themselves killed for nothing.

"I thought they got arrested for it. The cops, I mean," I said.

He pulled again at his hair.

"Arrested?" he said sarcastically. "They were cleared at a hearing. Murdered two innocent Mexicanos and restored to duty at full pay a month later. Do you call that justice?"

I shook my head, wondering was the Dummy still waiting where I put him?

"No, sir," I said. "But . . . "

His eyes were shining, his voice trembled, and he banged the table with his fist.

"The brown community cannot be treated like dogs," he said. "First of all we are men. We owned this state of California long before the Anglos stole it away from us. Don't you ever wonder why I live here in the barrio? Hasn't it ever entered your mind to think why is it that Mr. Alvarado, my English teacher, lives there in the barrio? Hasn't it?"

"Well, sure. As a matter of fact, I . . ."

"Solidarity," Mr. Alvarado said. "I choose to remain with my own kind. These are my people. Their lot is my lot."

"Okay," I said. "Sure. I dig that. But what about . . . ?"

I wanted to remind him of the things he said that day he didn't like my report on the Dummy and made me feel so small and cheap, but I decided against it. I shook my head and switched the subject.

"So what do you think I ought to do, Mr. Alvarado? You know—about—him."

He glanced at me as if surprised to see me still there.

"The first thing you'll do, of course, is get him out of the barrio. I can't afford to get mixed up in anything like this. It would cost me my job. Understand? They'd drop me like a hot potato. The Board would be only too happy to make me a scapegoat. I'm the only Chicano with tenure in the entire school district. And I've got to protect my fellow Chicanos, too. Get him away, do you hear? That's the first thing you must do. What you're doing is wrong. It's against the law."

I could hardly hear my own voice. "Yes, sir."

His finger wagged under my nose.

"And be very careful about it, very careful. Make very sure you're not seen with him in this neighborhood by any of the Los Angeles police. They'd start raiding every house immediately as an excuse to dig up suspects. My God! Something like this could set us back ten years—lose us all we've been fighting for."

"Yes, sir."

I was now at the door anxious to get away. He came close again, eyes boring down into mine intently.

"Get him back to where you found him. Where he belongs. Then contact the police. Do you hear? That boy must be given over to the proper authorities at once! It's for his own protection, too."

He threw the door open. As he did, Mrs. Alvarado came out of the bedroom. I could hear the kid coughing in there. She looked at me kind of surprised as I stepped through the doorway.

"Thanks a lot," I told Mr. Alvarado. "I hope your baby gets better soon."

He nodded grimly. "Thank you."

He closed the door and I heard him walking away.

I went down the stairs slowly, not sure any more about what he'd been saying to me, only sure that I was never going to come to Mr. Alvarado again for any kind of advice.

When I got to the bottom step I looked around. The Dummy wasn't there.

I started running.

I ran for two blocks. He wasn't anywhere in sight. I started to eat myself out for being such a dope as to leave him alone all that time. Considering Mr. Alvarado's reactions, I realized I was right not to take him up with me, but what should I have done? *You should have tied him up, you dope!* I said to myself, and ran faster, my heart beginning to pound in my chest.

I couldn't believe all that junk of Mr. Alvarado's about giving the barrio a bad name, but just the same it worried me. I knew they had a tough time down here and I didn't want to make it any worse.

Then I heard the sound of a drum around the next corner. And there he was, marching in a circle, followed by about a dozen little Chicano kids half his size, all clapping their hands in time as he beat his little drum.

Big house   Walk up big house   Inside big house.
Oh how funny . . . Big house go bump bump bump
Nice ride in big house bump-bump.

Don't worry now   all okay.   Okay   Okay.

Bump-bump house   no more   bump bump.
Come on out   do you hear . . . . . . now we got to go.

Want eat   Hurt here . . . . . . my . . . what.
Want-things-here-in-my-what
Hit hit my red boom boom.
What?

16

It's too bad Mr. Alvarado didn't see how nicely the Dummy and the little Chicano kids were getting along. Maybe he wouldn't have worried so much.

The kids all shouted, "No, no, Anglo!" when I walked up and pulled him away. I didn't blame them. I spoiled their fun.

I bawled the Dummy out for leaving after I had told him to stay put, but judging from that blank expression of his I knew I wasn't getting through.

Now what was I going to do? According to Mr. Alvarado I had to leave the barrio neighborhood right away, so I headed for the barrio bus stop. When we got there I put my hand in my pocket to see if I had the right change, and got a big surprise. All I found was a big hole.

I grabbed the Dummy's arm and ran back a few blocks, searching the ground. He didn't understand, of course, and clapped his hands and beat his drum thinking we were playing his game of looking at things. I couldn't find the money anywhere. And the more worried I got the happier the Dummy was, pointing out things he thought I'd missed.

I remembered sitting down briefly in Mr. Alvarado's apartment while he was laying things on the line and wondered if the money had slipped out of my pocket there. But I couldn't see going back, somehow. He probably wouldn't even open the door for me a second time, and if I told him I'd lost some money he'd think I was putting him on, trying to hit him for a loan. The chances were it had fallen out of my pocket while I was running along looking for the Dummy, or maybe earlier on the bus, the last time I'd needed to use money. Wherever, it was sure gone now. You didn't lose money in a poor neighborhood with a lot of hungry kids and expect to ever see it again. Besides, who could blame them for a lunkhead's hole in his pocket?

The Dummy was squatting over a manhole cover cocking his head and saying, "Nice, nice." How could I break the news to him that we were dead broke, a long way from home, and no means to travel?

A black-and-white prowl car turned the corner. That woke me up, even though it turned the other way. I grabbed the Dummy's arm and moved him along fast in the opposite direction. I didn't know if they were looking for us but I couldn't take any chances. A lot of kids knew I was some kind of friend to the Dummy and, even if they hadn't seen us running off together, might have told the cops who to look for.

A lot of things in this neighborhood looked different and interesting to the Dummy and I had to keep at him to keep moving. He really was a heavy lump. I was getting tired of pushing and pulling him. On top of being worried and scared I suddenly started feeling hungry. I figured if I was, then so was he. So now we had another problem coming up—like what to do about food. It was getting to be around dinner time and I could picture my family all sitting down at the table. There would be the questions about where was Neil. They might start leaning on Susie and, if she was worried about me, she might tell what happened. After the way my folks had raved the other time, before anything had even happened, I could imagine how they would go on about it now with some little girl hurt. My old man would hop to the phone and get the P. D. in a flash, giving them all the news about his son being with a loose maniac brain-damaged kid they knew was dangerous from the start.

I felt tired and discouraged and like dropping the whole thing. And then we rounded the corner and I saw this big white Bekins moving van parked along the curb and two husky guys wearing the white coveralls they all use loading it with furniture. I was ready to move up close with the Dummy the next time they walked back into the house for another load. The van was almost full. I knew in a little while the moving men would be back with the rest of the stuff, throw it inside, lock up, and off they'd go. I didn't have any idea where they were going but any place seemed a good idea right then. I grabbed the Dummy's arm.

"Come on," I told him.

He let me pull him up the board ramp leading into the open side of the van. It was packed tight, but I climbed and had him climb over a lot of boxes and chairs and tables until we were in the back.

There was a big sofa there and a stuffed chair with just enough room for us, and I pushed the Dummy down and cautioned him to keep quiet by putting a finger across my lips.

He repeated my action with his finger and bobbed his head happily. We were hemmed in on every side by all kinds of household goods and furniture and the Dummy smiled and pointed to the chair I was on.

"My . . . my . . . " he said, probably thinking it was like his own home, a crowded mess.

In a little while the two moving men returned to push a tall carton up the ramp on their little hand truck, set it in place and adjust some padding over some things in the section near the opening.

"I guess that does it, Al," the husky blond man said. The other nodded and they jumped off, put the ramp inside and slid the big side door shut.

The Dummy was sitting just across from me and now it suddenly became so dark inside I couldn't see his face. A lock snapped into place outside and in a few moments the engine started. We began to move off slowly, some of the furniture and boxes shifting slightly and shaking as we rumbled away, picking up speed.

"Oh how funny," the Dummy said. "Big house bump bump."

I never expected that being a stowaway in a moving van would remind me of home, but I had the same feeling. All that we needed was a couple of lighted lamps, then some sandwiches and soft drinks. My stomach reminded me of them. I began to wonder when and where the next stop would be. As I pushed some more things away, trying to make myself comfortable, the Dummy began beating his drum.

"Boom boom. Bump bump. Boom boom. Bump bump," he said, in cadence.

I wanted to shut him up at first, afraid the men in the cab up front might hear. But there were so many other loud noises inside the van as the furniture and boxes shifted and bounced I changed my mind. The men were too far away from the back corner where we were. Let him enjoy himself, if that was all it took. He certainly didn't seem worried about a thing.

I wondered about the way he trusted me, not asking where we were going, or why, or fussing. He seemed not to care. That was the main thing that bugged me about the Dummy. Didn't he think or have any feelings at all?

I know I worry and brood too much about a lot of things. It's a curse, but still better than not caring about anything, any more than a vegetable. How would it be not to care about things, not to get mad?

The more I thought about it, the more I wondered was I doing the right thing helping him run away. It was one thing to be trusted, but altogether different in his case because he couldn't think straight, if at all. To have somebody like that dependent on you struck me as a little like stealing. What if I messed up his life by leading him wrong? He needed help all right, but he needed it from somebody a lot smarter than I was.

Who would that be, if I had the same kind of present problem he had? Now that Mr. Alvarado had turned out to be something of a fink, who was there to turn to? I thought and thought about it while the furniture in the big van rumbled and swayed and the Dummy beat on his drum and chanted the same words over and over again, and I couldn't think of anybody. I thought of my sister Susie a couple of times, but she was only a little kid and I knew the main reason my brain kept coming back to her was because it couldn't come up with anybody else.

I knew a lot of kids would be calling their folks, one parent or the other and sometimes both, and say *look, I'm in a kind of jam and it's something I can't figure out and what do you think?*

I remembered Charley once got picked up for stealing another kid's bicycle. I mean, he really didn't mean to keep it, only ride on it awhile, say a day or so, then give it back and have the other kid wonder where it had been all that time. The cops let him call his folks from the station house and explain that, and they came right down and talked it over with the other kid's folks and the desk sergeant and he was let go. They never even punished him. He got fed and talked to as usual.

The other kid's folks held no particular grudge but thought Charley ought to be punished. Charley's old man said he'd already been punished enough, caught doing what he thought was a smart-ass thing, and been honest enough to admit it. The other kid's parents still wanted him punished so he'd remember. But Charley's old man stood firm; he was sure his boy would remember it just fine, and it wasn't the end of the world, nothing malicious, just a harmless sort of prank that backfired. That ended the matter and Charley never had to pay for his crime.

Dave was another with pretty good folks. He once threw a waterbag down from the balcony of the local movie and it conked somebody on the head. He was dragged out by the manager who sent for the fuzz. His folks came down to the station house too and talked to the man who had caught the waterbag on his head. He had a big bump on his nose too—those waterbags actually can do a lot of damage. But he saw how scared Dave was and remembered some of the things he used to do when he was a kid, and when Dave told him how sorry he was, the man said all right, forget it. Dave and his folks thanked him for being a good sport and that was the end of that, too. I mean, according to Dave, his folks never ate him out about it again. They trusted him. So he watched himself after that and never threw another waterbag.

I happen to know a lot of kids who have done something pretty stupid at one time or another. I'm not saying I never did. All I'm saying is they were lucky enough to have the kind of parents who didn't break their arm for some dopey thing they'd done without thinking. I've often wondered what kind of a kid my old man was when he was about my age. I can't even imagine it. I get a feeling sometime he must have skipped his whole childhood and gone directly to being a grown-up.

I got to thinking then about the Dummy and what kind of life it must have been for him so far, and had to admit that bad as I thought my life was his had to be worse. I mean, my old man wasn't some kind of psycho put away behind high brick walls and my old lady could be pretty pleasant when she felt like it. I tried to put myself in his place with his kind of bringing up, the setup of the sister who wouldn't or couldn't talk, the sloppy housekeeping and nobody to talk to. Right away I saw that was no way to live. Even if you had a good brain to start with, under those conditions pretty soon you'd start losing the use of it because it would only get in the way.

The padded household goods in the big moving van bumped and shook, the Dummy kept beating his drum and singing the same song he started with, and after a while my head started nodding and I dozed off. The last decent thought I could remember thinking was how comfortable and safe me and the Dummy were, and this ride would last forever.

141

No more big house
Oh what what?
My number-one boy mad-no-no face.
What the hell you Dummy you ... don't you know
what ...   don't you know they will ...
What's the matter with . . . . . you-you-you-you-you.
Cut it out now I said.   Will you . . . . .   you ...

Oh oh how very
Now-you-can't   now-they-won't   now-we-will . . .
You   you   you ...
My very red thing ...   boom boom stick ...
Oh what are you ...

Why   no   more   hit   my?

17

I'm in big trouble. I thought I knew how to handle him. It was a terrible mistake. I'm sure I had to do what I did but it just didn't work out the way things are supposed to when you feel you're doing right. Maybe it's not such a hot idea at that, to feel so very certain. With other people, if you made a mistake there are ways to fix things up, come to an understanding. But you can't with the Dummy.

If he only wasn't such a Dummy!

Not long after I dozed off in the big Bekins moving van, I woke up with a start feeling all goose pimply. Something was wrong. I couldn't tell what, at first, then I noticed the awful quiet. The Dummy had stopped beating his drum, and the furniture wasn't shaking and the van wasn't growling and rumbling.

"No more go," the Dummy said. "No more go, no more go."

He was right. The van had stopped. And then I heard the big side door being unlocked. Wherever we were supposed to go, we had arrived. In another moment the moving men would start unloading. I grabbed the Dummy's hands.

"Hold it now," I told him. "No more drum. We got to wait."

He didn't understand and struggled to get his hands free.

"My . . . my . . . " he said, trying to hit his drum.

The side door was sliding back. There wasn't any time to argue so I slapped his hands and whispered, "No, not now!"

He started to say something and I put my hand across his mouth. He tried to jerk loose. I turned him around and got one hand over his shoulder and covered his mouth to keep him from yelling, while I held on to his hands with my other hand. He was strong and I had to use all my might.

"Hold it, for Pete's sake," I whispered in his ear. "Just hold it."

He tossed his head back, banging me across the nose. I saw stars. I held him closer, hoping he'd catch on and relax. I didn't dare whisper any more, just gripped him hard.

The moving men were letting down the side ramp. Then one of them started toward a house in the distance while the other loosened a few straps and threw aside the big padded blanket coverings. Then he too jumped down from the van and followed the first Bekins man.

I strained after his fading footsteps until I couldn't hear them. I took my hand off the Dummy's face and pushed him away from me.

"Okay," I said softly. "They're out of sight now. This is our chance. Let's go."

He turned to look at me, bobbed his head and smiled. Then he lifted his drumsticks and brought them down on the drum.

"Boom!" he said happily.

I felt like murdering him. I did grab the drumsticks from his hands.

"Not now," I told him. "Maybe later."

He didn't understand, he simply held his hands out for them. While I cocked my head to see if the men were returning, he grabbed for the drumsticks. I smacked his hands and then the top of his head.

"Cut it out!" I scolded. "We got to go now. Come on."

I yanked him to his feet, and dragged and pushed him around and over the furniture. He was like a dead lump. I had to use all my strength to get him to the opening. Then I pushed him down the ramp, got him going with me beside him, pulling him along.

"Come on. Lift your feet. We got to move fast."

He looked at me, then at the drumsticks I was still holding.

146

"My . . . my," he said, extending his hands. "Things. Hit things."

We were about fifty yards away from the house on a quiet dark street. Lights were on in most of the houses. Some cars were parked along the curb but I couldn't see anybody. It was night but I didn't know what time it was and I still didn't know where we were. I knew I couldn't keep dragging the Dummy forever, so I decided to explain once more and then take a chance.

"No hit things now," I told him. "Not now. Later. Understand?"

"Aaaah," he said.

I shook my head. "You can't play it now," I said. "Can't you get that into your head?"

He looked at me blankly, then down at his open hands. He turned them over and looked at the backs of them. He just didn't get it. I put the drumsticks into my back pocket.

"Come on," I said. "Let's take a walk. Okay? Look at things. Okay?"

He looked only at the drumsticks in my pocket and showed me his hands again.

"My things," he said.

I took his arm and started urging him along.

"Later," I told him. "Later you can play it all you want. Not now."

"Now," he repeated. "Now now now."

I shook my head. "Not now. Not now."

His head bobbed. "Not. Not not. Not not not."

"You got the idea," I told him. "Not. Not now."

"Now now now," he said, starting to jump up and down.

I was hoping he would think of something else because I was running out of ways to explain our situation. I looked up and down the street. I knew I'd never been in this section before though it still looked familiar. The houses were mostly Spanish with tile roofs, better than average, a little bigger, and there were palm trees at intervals farther down the block. That told me something. At least we were still in California. The night air seemed the same as in my neighborhood.

The Dummy looked about to cry. "My. My things."

I'd never known him to have a tantrum before but he seemed ready for one now. I wished I knew where we were and what I was going to do with him. I never did have a plan. Maybe that was why everything started falling apart so quickly later. I was afraid right then if he started really making a fuss, yelling and screaming, that would be more reason for worrying than trying to pacify him by letting him have the drumsticks.

We were approaching an intersection with a lot of street traffic. He was getting more and more balky, reluctant to move a step, and I was getting tired of pulling. I didn't know whether the cops were looking for us, or had an all-points bulletin broadcast like they do to pick up on sight one kid and another with a drum. I figured somebody in that dumb mob outside of his house must have squealed. I waved my arm around generally to include the whole neighborhood.

"Look," I told him. "Look at all the pretty things."

He tugged at my shirt instead, beating at my chest with his fists.

"My . . . my . . . hit things," he cried.

I stopped short of the corner. Cars were zipping by on the wide boulevard but I didn't see any black-and-white prowl cars. I patted the Dummy's hand.

"Okay," I told him. "But listen, will you? I'll give you the sticks—your hit things—but you don't hit your drum now. Understand?" I took the sticks out of my pocket, put them near his drum and shook my head. "No play now. No hit now. Okay?"

He didn't take his eyes off the drumsticks.

"How about it?" I asked him. "Okay? Will you be nice now if I give them to you? No play now. Okay?"

His head bobbed and he smiled greedily.

"Okay. Okay."

He held his hands out wide, palms up. I put the sticks on them and closed his fingers around them.

"Okay," I said. "Just hold them now. No playing."

He looked at his hands and saw the sticks in them and he broke into a broad smile. "My . . . my!" Then he swung his arms apart and before I could stop him he had brought his hands and drumsticks down on the drum as hard as he could, chanting, "Boom Boom Boom!"

149

Nobody opened a door and came after us, but I panicked. I grabbed his hands angrily and twisted the drumsticks out of them.

"You Dummy!" I yelled into his face. "I told you not to! Don't you understand? They'll be looking for somebody like you playing this stupid drum!"

I took the drumsticks and snapped them in half over my knee and threw the pieces away. Then I ripped the drum off his neck, breaking the strap. I'd forgotten the sound he used to make. I heard it again as I put my fist through the thin drumhead, then dropped it on the ground, turned it over, and put my foot through the other side. I was too mad to stop now. I put it on end and stepped on it with all my weight. That flattened one side. I did the same to the other, then picked it up and showed it to him. A twisted flattened piece of broken tin.

He made a sound like I'd cut off his right arm.

"Aaaah!"

"Well, I warned you," I said, and scaled the flattened tin across the street. He watched it go, open-mouthed. "That takes care of that problem," I told him. "We got enough worries without it. Now come on."

I grabbed his arm to pull him along and he surprised me by going along without word or sign of protest. I was so mad I was shaking, but after taking another look at him I felt I had to explain.

"It's for your own good," I said. "I'm trying to save your neck, don't you see?"

He didn't answer. He didn't even look back for his drum.

"While I'm at it," I continued, "I'm sorry I had to smack you back there in the moving van. But it's for the same reason. When you're trying to hide, you can't make any noise. Don't you know that?"

His face didn't have any expression on it at all. I heard a funny sound and didn't know what to make of it. It continued at intervals and then I knew what it was. The Dummy wasn't moving his lips, or showing any tears, but the sound he was making was a moaning sound, as if he was crying inside. It was like his "Aaah" sound, only coming from inside him.

I knew now I'd made one big mistake about him. He was a Dummy, all right, but I knew now he had feelings. It didn't make me feel any better to discover that.

18

The broken drum strap dangled on the Dummy's neck. I thought he might notice it, that it would remind him of his broken drum and he'd go to pieces again. I slipped it off, rolled it up and put it into my pocket. He didn't appear to notice, just kept walking along like he was in a trance. I had to stop him when we came to the corner or he would have stepped right out into the moving traffic. He still continued that odd short moaning sound, a soft sighing hum.

"It was only a drum, for Pete's sake. I'll get you another one tomorrow. Honest."

I really meant to. They didn't cost too much, and I thought maybe my pop could help me get one cheap. Then I realized how dumb that was. Because what would he do to me when I got home for staying out all night? I didn't have any long-range plans, like staying away from home for good, or running away with the Dummy. It was just a matter of time, getting through the problem of our present situation. I couldn't even think of going home until I knew the Dummy was safe.

I wished there was some way of talking to my kid sister Susie and explaining what the problem was. Sometimes, even though she was only a little kid, she could come up with some pretty good answers. I remembered what happened right after I gave the Dummy the drum. More people heard him in the next twenty-four hours than ever knew he was alive before.

Susie tipped me off first.

"Boy, of all the dumb ideas!" she said. "Why did you give it to him?"

I pretended I didn't know what she was talking about.

"What d'ya mean?"

She looked at me as if I had just come down from another planet.

"You know what I mean. Boom boom boom. That's what."

"Oh," I said. "The drum, you mean."

"He's going around driving everybody crazy with it. You've got to do something."

"What can I do?"

She shrugged. "You gave it to him, didn't you?"

"Sure."

"Then take it back or something."

"But I can't," I had told her. "He'd never understand."

"Okay, then," she said. "It'll be on your head."

"What do you mean—on my head?"

"I mean, if somebody kills him to shut him up."

I shook my head. There was no way I could do anything and she knew it.

"Maybe he'll get tired of hitting it."

"Yeah," Susie said. "Sure he will."

As it turned out, she had practically guessed right. Only I was the one who nearly killed him to shut him up. Of course, I didn't actually kill him, but taking his drum away and deliberately breaking it was almost like putting an end to him. It was funny, too, when you consider that I was the one trying to help him.

I tried to get a good grip on myself and focus on what I had to do. There wasn't any sense in two zombies walking around all night. I was hungry and I knew he had to be hungry, too. Then a few blocks away I saw a big supermarket sign. A supermarket! Food! I grabbed the Dummy's arm and started pulling him along faster.

"Come on," I told him. "Maybe we can get something to eat there. Then we'll both feel better."

He let me pull him across the street. He wasn't any bother. He didn't show any interest, either, just kept on going with that glazed look like somebody had hit him over the head with a club, and softly sighing to himself every other time he set his left foot down, like it had a wire attached to a button in his head. One—two—three—hum. One—two—three—hum.

155

I glanced up automatically at the street sign. I'd seen it before, and suddenly I knew where we were —Lawnville, one of the many little towns strung out along the coastal highway, part of Los Angeles county, and not too far from Bellwood the section I lived in. Maybe an hour's ride unless you travelled by moving van, which took a little longer.

It cheered me up to know I wasn't too far from home, and I began to walk with a little more life. Until then I'd been awfully depressed, feeling like it was the end of the world. A sign in the sky over a bank flashed the temperature and time every few minutes: temperature 52, the time 8:48. I'd missed dinner at home by only 2 hours and 18 minutes. It had taken me only 5 hours and 33 minutes to become a fugitive, starting with the time Susie told me he was in trouble over the incident in the park. I began to count out my whole life as we walked toward the supermarket's neon sign that spelled out RIGHTWAY in red, and it came to 12 years, 7 months and 14 days. If the police were looking for me along with the Dummy I wondered was I one of the youngest fugitives or did somebody have me beat?

I hadn't done anything bad but then neither had the Dummy, so far as I could tell, yet here we were, both of us, uptight and on the run because of a lot of hotheads you couldn't talk sense to.

I began to look around me more carefully as we drew closer to the big parking lot of the market, one part of my brain worrying about statistics and sort of

156

feeling sorry for myself, the other part more practical and ready for an emergency. Somehow, even though we didn't have any money, I knew we'd be able to get something to eat at the supermarket.

RIGHTWAY, like a lot of the big chain stores in Southern Cal., usually closed at 9. I looked back at the lighted bank clock. The temperature was still the same but the time was now 8:52. That meant in less than 10 minutes all the cars would be out of the parking lot, and there would be fewer people to worry about who might have heard something over their car radios about being on the lookout for two dumb kids around 12 and 13. After the late shoppers left, the store clerks usually started throwing out their empty cartons and sort of getting the place in shape for the next day.

There was a shed around the side and I guided the Dummy toward it. I'd noticed before, while fooling around supermarkets, that they threw out a lot of stuff, like leaky milk cartons, egg boxes that were broken, cans bent out of shape, sometimes bread and cake too stale to sell, plus a lot of vegetables and fruit that got spoiled and they had to get rid of. There were usually two big metal containers with hinged tops near the shed, a delivery point for the food trucks, and they threw a lot of old unsalable food in there. And before getting to the shed, they just threw the boxes outside, leaving them there until some box boy stacked them in or alongside the metal containers for the garbage pick-up the next day.

I didn't want to be seen poking around while the

lights were still on so I led the Dummy to the dark alley nearby, and told him to sit down like me and wait, because we still had a little time to kill. He obeyed dumbly, let me push him down and leaned his head back against the whitewashed market wall. I did the same, trying to relax and not worry, but kept one ear cocked for the shoppers getting into their cars and driving off.

The Dummy had suddenly and mysteriously stopped the moaning sound but replaced it with an odd rocking movement, swaying back and forth and not caring when his head bumped the wall on its return. It seemed to me that even a brain-damaged kid could hurt himself that way and I told him to stop. He didn't let that break his rocking rhythm for a second.

"Cut it out," I said. "Don't you know you can hurt yourself that way? You'll scramble your brains."

He didn't seem to hear and kept right on, so I grabbed his arm and shook him.

"Stop it," I said directly into his ear. "Don't do that."

He turned his head and glanced indifferently at me and began another rocking motion.

"No!" I punched him on the arm. When he went back again I grabbed his hair and smacked him across the back of his head. "Cut that out, you Dummy!" I yelled in his ear.

He stopped immediately and looked at me.

"Aaah," he said

"Well," I told him, "I'm sorry, but somebody's got to look after you. I don't like to hit you but you got to stop banging yourself that way."

He slumped back against the wall and didn't say anything. I hated hitting him but as long as it worked I forgave myself a little. *I had to do it, didn't I?* I told myself.

I really wanted to cheer him up by telling him we'd soon be having something to eat, a big variety of different things, and maybe even some of that gooey cake he loved so much. But I was afraid of letting him down in case my master plan flopped, this just happening to be the one night in supermarket history when they didn't have anything spoiled or broken or unusable or unsalable.

"Everything will be okay soon," I told him, patting him on the arm. "Don't worry. The cops will have found whoever did that to the little girl, for one thing, and maybe tomorrow we'll be able to go home. So it's just a matter of overnight, see?"

I looked at him, hoping that he'd parrot even one little word the way he used to, one miserable syllable even, to show he was alive and didn't hate me. But he didn't. I kept on talking anyway.

"Your sister is probably okay, too, you know. I don't think that stone hit her too hard. A face always gets bloody when you get hit. I've had lots of bloody noses already from fights and ballgames. It's nothing serious. They probably took her to a hospital where they got good doctors. And if your mother worries, they'll probably find out where she works and tell her everything is all right."

He looked at me, then up at the sky, then let his head slump down between his shoulders.

"Hey, Alan," I asked him, and suddenly stopped, realizing that for the first time I'd addressed him by his name. He brought his head back up slowly. Maybe I was beginning to reach him again.

I heard wheels rattling in the parking lot, the sound of a shopping cart, and then a door opening and slamming and the sound of an engine. I glanced around the corner. There were still a few cars left, and the lights of the supermarket still on. I heard a door opening behind the wall and the loud sounds of boxes being thrown out. I looked up at the bank sign: 9:04, and the temperature had gone down two points. It was getting chillier all right, and I hoped those guys in the market would get on the ball and throw the things out the way they were supposed to, and then go home so I could get us something to eat.

There was still going to be some time to kill, though, so I tapped the Dummy's arm again to get his attention.

"How do you get along with your mother, Alan? Okay? I mean, I know she's very busy working hard so she don't have time to clean up your house, but how is she then; I mean, when she's home? Does she talk to you and your sister, and like that?"

He looked at me and I thought he shook his head slightly.

"That's what I figured," I told him. "I got the idea somehow that there wasn't any communication there. That she didn't like talking much. Is that true?"

He thought about it and then rubbed the back of his head where I'd hit him.

160

"How about your old man?" I asked. "I hear they got him put away in some kind of a mental home. Do you remember anything about him? Your father, I mean. You know his name?"

He bit his lip, then began rubbing the upper part of his arm where I'd punched him for banging his head against the wall.

"Okay," I said, "If you don't want to talk about it." I touched the short sleeve of his T-shirt. "Are you cold? I'm sorry about keeping you out so late. I guess if I'd known it was dropping down into the low fifties tonight, I'd have told you to put on a warm sweater or a windbreaker when we ran away from your house."

He rubbed both arms then, and that made me feel a lot better because I'd only hit him on one. Then I remembered I'd smacked him a few times in the moving van to get him under control, and all that good feeling went away.

"It's not just brain-damaged kids that have trouble with their folks," I told him. "Just strictly between the two of us, and without mentioning any names, I got two rotten eggs for parents. I don't like either one of them and both of them hate me, so maybe you're not as bad off as you think."

He looked at me curiously. *Maybe it was the word eggs. The food level seems to reach him easiest.*

I tried to remember how long my folks and I hadn't been getting along, and it seemed like always. I tried hard to remember when it began and why. I was now the oldest and usually the oldest isn't treated too badly,

161

especially if he's the only living son. Then suddenly I remembered something from way out of the past, so long ago I'd forgotten completely about it; I must have been an infant when I heard it. At first I didn't believe I was remembering it correctly, that maybe I was making it up. Then I heard their voices in my head and knew I was remembering right.

"If only the other one had lived," I heard my father say. "Danny would have been a fine boy."

"Well, we've got this one now," my mother answered. "Maybe the Lord is punishing us for our sins."

I couldn't believe it! I couldn't have been more than a year old at the time, and I swear I was in my crib when they were talking. It cleared up the mystery anyway. They hated me because I wasn't the firstborn. They never forgave me for living in place of my older brother who died when he was five!

I started to tell the Dummy about it, still listening to the store clerks toss out boxes and slam things around. We seemed safe enough and there wasn't anything else to do.

"My old man hated me even more when I grew up," I told him. "He always thought he was this great athlete and ball player. He used to come down to the ball field when I was playing with the guys and start to show us up by showing how good he was."

I remembered the time he wanted to show me how to pitch and said I should throw some hard ones to him. I didn't want to because he wasn't wearing a glove. He got mad and I finally told him why. He laughed until his face got red.

"I guess I can handle your kind of smoke, fella," he said. "C'mon. Let's see your high hard one."

I threw it and I guess he didn't think I could throw that fast. He pretended it didn't hurt but he walked away right after that and that night I saw him soaking his hand in ice and complaining to my mother that I threw one at him before he was ready.

I was laughing softly now while I told the Dummy about it.

"Then a couple of weeks later he showed up on the field again. This time he was going to teach us how to bat. I struck him out twice in a row and he got mad again and walked off. The last time he showed up was when he came around again to teach us how to field, and show us how to play first base. I hit the first ball back to him on a wicked hop and it hit him in the face before he could get his glove on it."

The Dummy surprised me by touching my arm.

"One," he said.

I didn't know what he meant.

"Huh?"

He touched me again.

"Number one."

I shrugged. "Okay, if you got to pee, go ahead. Nobody will mind."

He didn't get up so I guess he thought about something else.

"Getting back to my mother, she talks a lot better than yours, but it's not always just friendly conversation. She eats you up a lot with her tongue, you see. That's her way of getting even. She keeps coming back at you with something you thought happened too long before to remember. And she keeps at you with it like it happened five minutes ago."

"My number one," the Dummy said.

I realized suddenly the parking lot was quiet and I hadn't heard any cars moving out in a long while. I looked around the building. The overhead parking lights were out, the lot was deserted. The store window lights were still on, but they keep them on at night. I couldn't see anybody inside.

I stood up. The numerals on the bank sign read: 9:42 and the temperature had gone down to 48 degrees.

"Zero hour," I told the Dummy. I leaned over him in the dark alleyway. "Now, listen. You got to stay here. I'm going for some food behind the building. Over there, at the supermarket. Will you promise to wait?"

I knew I couldn't depend on him if I took him along. He might find something interesting to look at when it was time to run, or he might accidentally do the wrong thing. He didn't have his drum any more but he was liable to start singing or yelling or whatever came into his head. It made more sense to leave him behind while I went foraging for the junked food.

"My number one," he said again, bobbing his head.

"Will you wait?" I asked him. "I won't be too long."

"One, one," he chanted. "Hit. Throw. Kick-one. Hit-thing one."

"*Oh, Jesus,*" I thought. "*He's not with it. What if he gets up and just decides to leave?*"

I remembered the broken drumstrap in my pocket, and swiftly tied his ankles together with it.

"That will keep you around until Operation Breadbasket is finished," I told him. I put my finger warningly to my lips and moved away, secretly praying inside that I found some gooey cakes for him so he could say, "My . . . my!"

The loading shed was dimly lit by a light over the side door. I was lucky right from the start and saw more than I could hope to carry back in my bare hands. I found a carton and started throwing things from different boxes into it:

A half gallon carton of homogenized milk that smelled okay and just had a slight leak at the bottom. A cardboard carton of eggs, with only three cracked ones but two that were really ruined. Some tomatoes and apples too soft and spotted to sell, a bashed can of peaches, a cucumber, some carrots, radishes, and two ears of corn. A soggy split orange, some hairy potatoes, and a broken bottle of ketchup. I threw all that in, and kept looking.

There was so much stuff thrown out I actually had to reject some. A small can of tuna had me hung up for a while but I'd heard so much about the mercury problem I figured the heck with it. It would be just my luck to poison the Dummy accidentally with some supermarket leftover tuna fish. I threw back some more soggy fruit, and greens that were turning black. I had my mind set on finding some gooey cake for him, and just as I was beginning to doubt my luck I found a whole box of them—crumpled eclairs and cookies with a lot of melted chocolate syrup. I even found a lemon meringue pie. I didn't know if he liked that, but it looked so mushy I felt sure he'd flip when he saw it.

I jumped off the landing platform holding the full carton of food and started running for the alley. Suddenly out of nowhere I heard a man yell.

"Hold it, you—right there!"

I got scared and ran around some boxes, still holding on to my carton. I ducked around the alley wall and there he was, still sitting patiently.

I leaned down and slapped his shoulder.

"Come on—let's go! I got some food for us!"

He seemed slow in responding so I held the carton in one hand and jerked him up by his arm.

"Come on," I urged. "We got to make time now . . . run!"

I grabbed his arm and started pulling him along and he made a funny sound and stumbled.

"Pete's sake," I thought. *"What a Dummy! He can't even run when you want him to."*

Then a blinding light hit me in the eyes. I heard a man yelling for to come back. I let go of the Dummy's arm and started to run. I heard a shot and, right on top of that, another one awfully close. It never touched me, yet somehow I felt the bullet go right through me.

I turned around at a strange coughing sound and there was the Dummy flat on the ground.

"Oh how very bad," he said.

I looked down at the carton under my arm and saw

the broken bottle of ketchup still in there. Then this big security guard night-watchman type came running up.

He didn't have to grab me. I was already sitting on the ground talking to the Dummy, trying to tell him how sorry I was, that I'd forgotten I had tied his feet together with that damn drum strap.

19

I'm in a nice clean place where they smile and ask a lot of dumb questions. Like who I am, and don't I feel ready to go home now? Those are two of the dumbest.

The more I thought about everything, the more it seemed to make more sense to be like him. No reason why there couldn't be two Dummies, is there? No brains, no feelings. I'm going to try that. Instead of turning on, I'm turning off. Susie would understand, though it's more than trying one of her happenings.

I found out whatever I got it's not neurological. I heard one of the smiling people tell that to another smiley. I'm not even mentally retarded, for Pete's sake. I got some kind of altered personality due to an existing anxiety state from unknown psychogenic, I think, causes.

Hey Dummy, I thought. *Now this will teach you.* Even Mr. Alvarado didn't think it was catching.

Now this will teach you. Pay attention now, promise? Cut that out now. Will you listen to me? Please listen, Dummy.

My chest keeps getting too heavy. I feel okay but my chest is certainly too heavy. I may need a bigger chest. I think maybe I outgrew my old one.

169

Now it's my feet that feel funny. Not my head, like they think, but my feet, for Pete's sake. They feel like they're in the wrong place. I've been looking at my toes. They seem okay. One thing I notice is I sure have a lot of toes.

My left hand. Shoe. That. This. This shoe is. Sock. Hit. hit.

Susie . . . please . . . I . . .
I think I. Purple. Pink. People. Things.
What? Look. See. Walk. Look things. Look my things.
Here. There things. Air things up high.
Care. Air. No more care.

Tomorrow I am. Orrow. orrow. Are are are. oh oh oh. Eee eee eee. Ah ah ah.
Aaah. Who?
What if.
What

Aaaah.

Kin Platt's admirers are legion and the reasons for their admiration are six memorable books for young people, the latest of which is *Hey, Dummy*. The present book falls into the genre of *The Boy Who Could Make Himself Disappear*, the heartbreakingly-real story of Roger, who was confronted by emotional conflicts he had difficulty coping with. Roger's story is on its way to becoming a classic.

And there are his mystery stories *Sinbad and Me* and *Mystery of the Witch Who Wouldn't*, which feature Steve; his girlfriend, Minerva Landry (the sheriff's daughter); Sinbad, a wonderful English bulldog who doesn't talk but makes himself understood; and a variety of sinister characters. These were preceded by Kin Platt's legendary *Big Max* and *The Blue Man*.

In addition to his writing, Mr. Platt is a well-known cartoonist. His "Mr. and Mrs." and "Duke and Duchess" were known to thousands of readers before he gave up that phase of his career to devote himself exclusively to books.

An ardent golfer and devotee of physical fitness, Kin Platt spends part of each week in the gymnasium and on the golf course. He and his family live in Los Angeles, although he is equally at home in New York which was his home for most of his early life.